Sign up for our newsletter to hear about new releases,
read interviews with authors, enter giveaways, and more.

www.ylva-publishing.com

Other Books by Paulette Callen

The Charity Series

Charity
Fervent Charity

Epiphany

Stories, Essays, and Meditations on Animals

1 3 1644471 0

PAULETTE CALLEN

I have love for the footless,
for the bipeds too I have love;
I have love for those with four feet,
for the many-footed I have love.

-The Buddha-

For hundreds of thousands of years
The stew in the pot
Has brewed hatred and resentment
That is difficult to stop.
If you wish to know why there are disasters
Of armies and weapons in the world
Listen to the piteous cries
From the slaughterhouse at midnight.

-Ancient Chinese Poem-

I happily dedicate this book to Willow, a child who gives me hope for the future, and to Bodhi, a dog who gives me joy in the present.

Table of Contents

Acknowledgements

I AM GRATEFUL TO ALL the animals throughout my life who have comforted and inspired me and to all the people who taught me to be kind to them, starting with my grandfather Bill Magnus. He was unfailingly kind and gentle with all the neighborhood dogs who made their pilgrimage to our yard every day for the cookies he always carried in his pockets. In a place and time in which people often shot squirrels for fun or because they damaged property by getting into attics, he built boxes for them in our trees and kept the boxes filled with nuts and bread scraps all winter. Our squirrels were sleek and fat and never broke into an attic, garage, or outbuilding on our property.

Thank you, Doris Hess and Suzanne Schuckel Heath for your initial readings and helpful comments.

Thank you, Astrid Ohletz, founder of Ylva Publishing, for accepting the task of publishing these pieces—most of which have appeared in a variety of places over the years—as one collection.

Introduction

BEFORE WE HAD LANGUAGE, ANIMALS informed our dreams. Our first scribblings were of animals. They were our first gods, our sustenance, and the sum of most of our fears. Often these fears had nothing to do with the reality of the animal. [1] Even the fiercest predators have always had more to fear from us than we from them—proven by the fact that almost every apex predator but us is a threatened or endangered, if not already extinct, species.

Today, as discovered by those who have taken the time to see and listen to them, animals are proving to be more interesting than we have made them in our dreams and metaphors. They are valuable in and of themselves, not simply for what they do or signify for us.

Anthropomorphizing them doesn't elevate their status (compare, for example, the nobility of wolves providing for their young and old with humans' frequent abuse of their children and elders) but rather may cloud our understanding and appreciation for who and what they really are. Saying someone "behaved like an animal" no longer has any meaning to a thoughtful, knowledgeable person. Animals are not (with rare exceptions noted by Jane Goodall and others in their observations of wild chimpanzees who not infrequently make war on chimps from other groups) violent outside their imperatives to find food, mates, protect territory, and defend themselves. Getting drunk in a bar and going home to smash the furniture, smack the spouse and kids, and kick the dog is unique to humans; animals do not behave this way.

Some of the pieces in this collection were written years ago. Over time, I have mellowed in my approach but altered not a jot in my belief that we use and abuse animals to our peril, and that this is the most telling symptom of what is wrong with humans at our core. (Note that in the Genesis story, even before the blame for the fall of man was placed on a woman, it fell on an animal.) This belief is what turned me toward Buddhism a few years ago, not out of any religious fervor, but because the Buddha explicitly included animals in his circle of compassion.[2]

The stories, both true and fictional, the essays, and the musings in this collection are simply an offering, not to animals in the sense that I hold them as divine (any more or less than I hold all life sacred), but to the spirit of evolution that I hope envelops us all and will carry us toward a more peaceable kingdom.

---

1 *Bats, for example, still inspire fear and violent responses from people, to the point of making many of their kind extinct; and yet the bat herself is a winsome, shy, affectionate, exquisitely clean, and ecologically necessary being. Without her, our skies would darken with insects and many of our plants, from trees to food crops, would not be pollinated. The bat is a close relative of primates; yes, if chimpanzees (chimps and humans share 96 percent of the same DNA) are our brothers and sisters, the little bat is our second cousin.*

2   *Christianity has within it the seeds to be a leader in compassion and respect for animals, but established churches have not seen fit to encourage those seeds to grow. Andrew Linzey, an Anglican priest who has written a number of excellent books about Christianity and animals, maintains that if we understood the heart of the Christian message, which is the sacrifice of the higher for the lower, we could not abuse and use animals the way we do. We could not sacrifice them in our laboratories or our slaughterhouses. We would care for them, nurture them, protect them, and love them, the way our God demonstrated His love for us.*

A little passage in The Gospel of Thomas—*a document purportedly rejected for the New Testament Canon by the early church men (those same men that tried to make of Mary Magdalene a prostitute, though nothing exists in any scripture to support that notion) quotes Jesus as saying, "Split a piece of wood, and I am there. Lift up the stone, and you will find me there." What do you find when you split a piece of wood? What do you find when you lift a stone? The smallest, humblest, most unsung creatures of our earth. The tiny, crawling, scampering, or wiggling beings that hide their faces from the light. The beings, without whom, life would not be possible on this planet. This passage tells me that they, even they, are worthy of our respect and our mindfulness. And in this passage, Jesus tells us so.*

FICTION

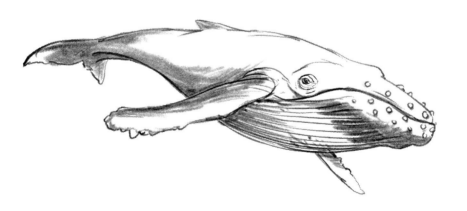

Satyagraha

YOU CAN TELL SAINTS, NOT by their miracles and thin faces, but by their smiles. St. Francis, I think, grinned from ear to ear at a sunbeam or a tree frog, at a child or a pope.

The Buddha smiles and is smiling still from Katmandu to Riverside Drive.

The whales smile beaming serenity in man-made charnel seas; diving and dancing around our bloody factory ships; singing their mantras while we dissect their stolen children; living and loving gently through our poisons, wastes, and wars; imprisoned, patiently playing our games; never repaying us in kind.

They are finally winning us over.

Epiphany

"DRESS FOR A MINNESOTA WINTER, Gram. Then you'll be warm enough on the boat," Kari had admonished her. "No matter how warm it feels on shore, once you're out there on the water, it's *cold*." Hildy had had eighty-three Minnesota winters during which to practice dressing. Cold she wouldn't be.

She took her time unpacking and arranging her things. She hated living out of a suitcase. She was all in from the trip. So much so, she nearly fell onto the bed without unpacking or doing anything other than taking off her shoes. She rested for a few minutes, then decided to get up and make a good job of it, so in the morning, she would not have to.

The train ride had been pleasant, but the last leg of the journey on that bone-rattling bus without a working lavatory was pure hell. "I'm going to write a thing or two to that bus company when I get home, believe you me," she muttered. She was so relieved to be here that she wasn't feeling her excitement yet. It lay dormant, shrouded by exhaustion. Years of dreaming about this trip, months of planning—what a fuss they had made! *A body'd have thought I wanted to go to the moon instead of the East*

Coast, for Pete's sake. She slammed the top drawer of the little motel dresser shut on her underthings, still annoyed with her daughters. Especially Leona: "What in the world do you want to go on a whale watch for, of all things, at your age?" Marion had been not much better, though not as vocal.

"At my age!" Hildy snorted. "*Now* is not the time to be putting things off." After carrying on to high heaven, they had finally accepted the idea and began making plans for her. Oh, the looks on their faces when she told them her plans were already made! She chuckled. They were especially put out when she declined the pleasure of anybody's company. Even Annie, her best friend. Even Kari. "The child is busy with her own life. What does she want to go traipsing off to Provincetown with an old lady for? Besides, she's already been there." And Annie couldn't go, even if she had wanted to (which she didn't) because she was moving into Hildy's apartment to look after Nick and Nora, Hildy's cats, who were too precious to be entrusted to her daughters.

Kari had met Hildy at LaGuardia and put her up for the night in her Lower East Side apartment. *What a horror!* Hildy thought when she first entered the shabby, cramped semi-basement. But the girl was a tidy housekeeper and seemed not to notice. "It's so dark!"

"It's a railroad flat, Gramma. I only have windows at the front and the back. You get used to it."

Hildy reminded herself that standards were different in New York City, and she said no more about the apartment. She did not want to be like Leona, Kari's mother, harping on every detail.

"Gram, if you wait a few days, I can go with you."

6

"I want to go alone."

"Why?" Kari wasn't challenging, just curious.

"This is something I've wanted to do for years. Don't fuss." *You're the only one I give a snap about, Precious.*

"You didn't tell Mom that you didn't book a return flight."

"No. She'd have had another fit. She likes to know the beginning, middle, and end of a thing before it happens. Why in Sam Hill do anything then?"

"She's going to be furious."

"Sweetheart, that's how I'll know I'm dead, when your mommy stops being mad at me."

Kari smiled a little. "What am I supposed to tell her when she calls?"

"Tell her the truth. I don't want you in hot water with her on my account. I'll be back when I'm good and ready. Now, Precious, make those calls for me. I don't hear so good over the phone."

Hildy took out a much-folded piece of paper from the side pocket of her purse and handed it to her granddaughter. "Amtrak is first, you see. Then the bus. The train only goes as far as Providence. Don't ask me why. The bottom number there, you see, is the motel. It's an inn or something like that. They have this package deal. I get a free whale watch for every weekend I stay there."

"What if they don't have any rooms? This is very short notice."

"My land, it's only May. They'll be empty. They'll be tickled pink to have me."

"How long do you want to stay?"

"As long as it takes. I don't expect whales to rally around the boat just because I'm on it."

"They have sightings just about every day in season, Gram."

"I don't want to just gawk at them like some yahoo. I want to meet them properly. And I want to see dolphins. Oh, land! I want to see dolphins. *They* don't come around every day. I can tell you that!" Hildy waved her finger in the air. "Make it for two weeks to start."

"This is going to be kind of expensive, isn't it?"

"I've planned for it. Don't worry. I have plenty of travelers' checks right here." Hildy patted the side of her purse. "I mean to use them all if I have to."

Kari was hesitant, but Hildy knew she'd make the calls. *You're nothing like your mother, thank the Lord.* Then she thought, *It's a good thing we mortal humans aren't yet telepathic. Whales and dolphins, they say, are.*

She found herself gazing at Kari, drinking her in, savoring every detail of this petite, brown-haired young woman, her only grandchild who, in looks, was a throwback to Ed...the curly, baby-fine hair, brown eyes, the small straight nose, and rosy skin. Leona would be harping on the girl's clothes. The long paisley skirt, the anklets and slip-on shoes, an oversized cardigan over a T-shirt. Her mother kept sending her shirtwaist dresses and A-line skirts, which Kari left at the thrift stores where she got most of her clothes. *Young girls aren't pressed and permed anymore, and it's a blame good thing*, thought Hildy. Anyway, Kari was cute as a bug no matter what she wore.

Hildy's eyes had blurred then. She fished in her purse for a tissue and took off her glasses to clean them. She could hardly see a blessed thing. She couldn't tell anymore if the glasses made things better or worse. Just different. The eyes were nearly gone, just like everything else.

She finished hanging up her shirts in the closet, including the wool Pendleton—still the warmest single thing she owned—that had been Ed's. Her pants and sweaters were folded in the bottom drawer of the dresser, and she put the empty suitcase in the back of the closet out of sight.

Then she took her overnight bag into the bathroom and drew a bath while she arranged her toothpaste, lotions, and dusting powder on the sliver of counter space around the sink. She was bone weary—more tired than hungry. She had raisins, peanuts, and an apple in her purse if she wanted something later. She smiled and shook her head. *Of all the foolishness.* A plane. A train. A bus. Then a cab to get here from the bus station. Tomorrow morning, the cab would carry her to the boat that would take hours to get to a place somewhere out in the ocean to see whales. *And, if I'm lucky, dolphins.*

Some excitement tingled through her aches and weariness. She had read that she could expect to see humpbacks here, perhaps a fin whale, although they were very shy and seldom came near a boat. And maybe dolphins. She took her empty overnight bag back to the bedroom and put it in the closet with her suitcase. Then she took off her sturdy sneakers and put them next to a pair much the same, but a half size larger so she could wear extra heavy socks inside them. She didn't want cold feet on the boat. She slipped into her Dearfoams, a present from Annie, and padded back into the bathroom.

Poor Annie. She didn't understand Hildy's wanting to take this trip any better than did her daughters. Hildy and Annie had been friends for—it felt like a hundred years.

Annie was her best friend, not because they shared interests, but because they were still alive and had known each other longer than anyone else they knew. They disagreed on most things. Annie fussed at Hildy constantly: her clothes were not ironed; she never went to the beauty parlor. "You know, they have senior citizen rates on Wednesday at A Cut Above on Hennepin. Jackie there does a nice job."

"Who cares about my blame hair? And I threw out the iron when I retired."

But mostly Annie worried for Hildy's immortal soul because she did not attend church anymore. "Well, if you don't like the church you went to, find another one. Minneapolis is full of churches, God knows. Find one of the crazy ones, where they wear sneakers and play guitars and things like that."

"I was baptized in a church, confirmed in one, married in one, and took my children till they were old enough to go on their own and had my mother's funeral in one. None of it did me a stick of good. It never made me happy. Do you want butter on your popcorn?" They settled in to watch the latest episode of *Murder, She Wrote*, one thing on which they did agree.

The tub was full. Hildy tested the water to make sure it wasn't too hot, undressed, and carefully lowered herself into the water. She had to be careful in everything she did. It was so tiresome. Though she pretended to her daughters that she didn't. Leona's ever mournful cry "What if she breaks a hip?" had become the family joke, she wailed it so often, whenever Hildy wanted to do anything. But Hildy knew it was no joke. Her body had been failing her, betraying her little by little over the years. She couldn't trust it. When the apostle said the spirit is willing but the flesh is weak, he was probably just talking about old age. Worst of all were her hands and wrists. "I can't even pick up my cast iron skillet anymore," she complained to Annie. "I had to give all my cast iron to Marion. Now I use these little aluminum things. I hate them. But—no strength left. Anyway, the only thing I fry nowadays is my pancakes. Don't taste any good without my skillet, but there's no help for that." She didn't even trust herself to pick up her cats. She always sat and let them jump on her lap for cuddling. She also had to be aware of balance in everything she did. Once her balance was lost, she knew there would be no catching herself, even if she had something to grab on to. Her wrists wouldn't hold her.

She soaked a few minutes to ease out the kinks and then scrubbed herself all over. She climbed out of the tub, carefully, and dried off with the motel towels that were much more luxurious than what she was used to, put on her bloomers, her undershirt, and slipped a flannel nightgown over it all. Then, even though there was plenty of light left, she crawled into bed settling back against the pillows to read for a while.

But she didn't read. She thought. This would be her last trip anywhere. She hadn't taken many in her life. Northern Minnesota when she was much younger. The Black Hills with her married daughters. She had enjoyed the scenery, except for Mount Rushmore. The wonder of that was not that some guy had carved those big faces into the side of the mountain, but that he had wanted to. Hildy couldn't see the point except to give someone the excuse to erect an unsightly tourist center across from it that sold cheap souvenirs and fast food. No, the best thing about Mount Rushmore was that Cary Grant movie.

This place was utterly different from any place she had been before. She got up and cranked open her window so she could get a room full of ocean air and hear the susurration of the waters, that, even on this windless evening, rose and fell, rhythmic as a pulse. She knew it wasn't just the wind that moved the seas, but currents and tides—the moon, maybe even the stars.

She sank into the blueness of this room: the faded blue walls, the dark blue carpet with its darker markings. The paint wasn't fresh, nor the carpet new, but she liked it. It was clean, simple, and right for this place perched on the edge of the world. The open-weave blue plaid curtains billowed inward and fell back. She pulled the blue cotton bedspread up and reached for her novel. Or perhaps she would just doze a little, then...

Something jangled in her ear. It took another two rings for her to orient herself and pick up the telephone.

"Hello? Mrs. Flanagan? This is your wake-up call."

"My land. What time is it?"

"Five o'clock, ma'am."

"In the morning?"

"Yes, ma'am."

A wake-up call! Now that was something. And it didn't cost anything extra, either. Kari had told her to ask for one at the desk when she checked in, and it was a good thing, too.

She still felt her weariness upon her like a heavy blanket and knew she was not going to be up and out on a whale boat this day. She relaxed and slept several hours more. At 8:00 she got up, dressed, and found her way to the motel restaurant. The restaurant was not large, but through the plate glass windows she could see ocean and sky and seabirds riding the winds and scooping their own breakfasts from the sea. She ordered coffee and waffles. A nice change from pancakes.

She spent the day napping, reading, and sitting on one of the benches scattered on the manicured lawn in front of the Sea Scape Inn, which was the name of her motel, enjoying the frolic of waves, birds, clouds, and light. The Sea Scape was a modest place. She liked it for its hominess, the friendliness of the folks who worked here, and the fact it was so close to the water. She was tired but deeply content. She had the feeling that this place had been waiting for her.

For lunch, she ate her raisins and the apple outdoors, buttoned up in her Pendleton. For supper, she went back to the restaurant and ordered the chicken soup. It came with toast and a small salad and she enjoyed every morsel. By nightfall, when she again stepped out of her warm bath, she was feeling just pleasantly tired; she remembered to ring the desk for another wake-up call and went to bed.

When the 5:00 call came, she dressed and found the card the cab driver had given her: "Marvin...the only cab in town," which was literally true. During the drive from the bus station to the motel, he had been over talkative for Hildy's taste, but he'd carried her luggage in, refused a tip, and just before he left, had handed her his card. "Call me anytime," he said winking, which annoyed her further. "Special rates for senior citizens." Hildy took the card and sniffed. *He's no spring rooster himself.* Still, she appreciated the special rate. She dialed his number.

The wharf, almost at the other end of town, was like a street on stilts projecting far out over the water, a far cry from any of the docks she had known in Minnesota, even on the biggest lakes she had visited. It was so wide that, even with the small buildings along either edge, there was room for motorized traffic. She walked straight down the middle of it. This early there was very little activity. Seagulls squatted in various places over the dock, some at rest on the top of poles and coils of rope. One concession selling hot coffee and chowder was already open. Some places seemed to sell bait and tackle; some, those without signs, were perhaps privately owned. She didn't know where to go, but she kept her eyes open. *I'll see other people boarding a boat or something. I'll just ask.*

She didn't have to. Soon enough she saw a small crowd of people ahead, tickets in hand, parkas and jackets slung over their shoulders, gathered in front of a ticket booth not much bigger than a phone booth. Above it, the words **DANCER FLEET** emblazoned in blue on a white board sawed in the shape of a waving banner identified this as her fleet. Beyond it were two more ticket booths, similar to this one but in different colors and not yet open for business. She couldn't read their names, but it didn't matter. According to Kari, the Dancer Fleet was the best. The captains cared more for the comfort and safety of the whales than the convenience and curiosity of their passengers. They never moved in too close or too fast, and if there was already a boat zeroing in on one or more whales, they passed by. Fortunately for them and for the whales, their reputation attracted more passengers than it repelled.

Hildy exchanged her motel coupon for a ticket and stopped to look around again before boarding. Now she was exhilarated. The smells out here on the wharf were decidedly fishy and salty, unlike anything she had ever smelled. The Midwest was earthier, grassier, even around the lakes. Only the piping of the gulls was familiar, for she had heard a similar piping when she and Ed had been to Lake Superior the summer before Leona was born. She didn't want to think of that now. It was grand to be in a place that looked and smelled different, where there were few associations with familiar things. Everything was fresh and new and she felt almost as if she didn't have a past or that she could choose any past she liked, it didn't matter. What mattered was here and now, and she liked that feeling very much.

She felt her back straighten a little as she boarded the boat. On its side was printed *Wave Dancer*. According to the brochure she was given at the inn, there were five boats in the Dancer Fleet. She loved their names. *Rainbow Dancer*, *Star Dancer*, *Wind Dancer*, *Blue Dancer*, and her boat today. *Good names for cats*, she thought, and she wondered how Nick and Nora were getting along without her. The brochure said that only two boats a day went out for public whale watches. At other times, the boats were used by researchers to study the whales and, all too frequently, to rescue whales entangled in plastic fishing nets, no longer a rare occurrence as the oceans became a dumping ground for the nets of the fishing industries of many nations. Hildy had stopped eating seafood when she read of the carnage produced by this "ghost fishing."

"What good's that going to do?" Annie had fussed the first time Hildy refused to eat her fish sticks.

"Maybe no good. Maybe a lot. I don't know. But my conscience is clean. Besides, I won't take food out of the mouths of the creatures I love. I can eat something else. They can't."

"What about the cats? You still feed them cat food. That has fish in it."

"I know. I do what I can. Nobody's perfect. Make me a pancake."

Hildy remembered she hadn't had breakfast yet, so she went inside the cabin, fragrant with brewing coffee, clam chowder, and frying eggs. She read the menu on the blackboard (fortunately white-chalked in giant letters): Egg McDolphin, Danish, doughnuts, bagels, and rolls. For lunch there would be sandwiches and chowder, more coffee, and pop (though here they called it "soda"). No one would starve. She ordered coffee and a Danish. She believed this was the best coffee she had ever tasted and suspected the cold sea air made it so.

Coffees warm in hand, people settled themselves around the boat, inside and out, on upper and lower decks, while Moby, the captain's Newfoundland dog, bounded everywhere, ingratiating himself with all the passengers.

A young woman took the microphone on the lower deck close to where Hildy sat. She introduced herself as Carol, a marine biologist and their guide for today. Her black, curly hair was red-tipped from sun and salt. Her skin was baked brown, with deep lines around her eyes. Hildy guessed she was not yet thirty and aging fast in the sun—but for a good cause. Her voice carried throughout the boat as she explained whale biology and behavior. She knew her stuff, but Hildy paid no attention. She had read books on whales. Their singing, their migrations, care of the young, baleen, their big brains...it was all old news. Except... Hildy pricked her ears when she heard the question posed by another passenger. If it hadn't come up, she might have asked it herself, just to hear the answer. Not, *Why* do whales sing? (*Why does anybody sing?* thought Hildy. *It's fun.* She thought that was a stupid question, though the songs probably had something to do with mating, as only the males were thought to do it.) But, *How?* Carol, bless her, gave the right, the wonderful, the simple and beautiful answer: "We don't know." She told the wide-eyed whale watchers that no mechanism had been found in a whale that would produce sound and they did not apparently need an outgoing breath to produce sound the way land animals did. "We just don't know," Carol said again. Hildy felt some goose bumps at the thought that a bit of magic remained in the world and it was to be found in the sea, and she would soon come face to face with it.

Hildy took a seat and settled in to enjoy the steady forward motion of the boat. She was, at last, on the ocean. She tried to comprehend its vastness and found her mind emptying out and expanding till she was almost in a pleasant trance. She also experienced a deep peace, a remembrance of a childhood and adolescence spent on a prairie farm, where the land lay flat, unbroken by trees except those few planted by the early settlers around their houses for shade, the expanse of wheat or prairie grass waving in the wind under cloud-born shadows that ebbed and flowed over the fields with the ever-changing skies. The curve of the earth was visible, and a car or truck would emerge over the horizon on the dirt road leading up to their farmstead like a small ship at sea. And you could drown there too, almost, as she did when she was four or five and wandered into a cornfield and could not find her way out. The stalks of August corn, three times her height, closed in around her and she stumbled through them, crying until she heard her father's voice. "Hildy! Hildy!"

"Papa, Papa!" she had wailed and he had told her to stop right where she was and calm down. Then he said, "Okay, girl, keep talking to me now and don't move. I'll come and get you." And she kept saying, "Here I am Papa, here I am Papa Papa," and he followed her voice and picked her up and carried her out, back into the light. He just looked at her for a moment and set her down and said, "Okay, squirt. Now run home. Ma is waiting dinner for you. Tell her I'll be along." And he patted her bottom to see her off. She hadn't thought of her father in a long time.

The rhythmic hum of the boat's motor and the soft *shuushuushing* sound of the water parting around them eased her to her very bones. No wonder people went to sea. Occasionally someone would sit next to her and try to start a conversation. They were being kind to a cute little old lady alone on a boat. But she had had a lifetime of making conversation with people, most of whom she didn't care for. Now she wanted to be alone with the sea and its creatures. She was polite but reticent, and they soon wandered on to do their own sea viewing or to talk with their friends or fiddle with their cameras.

As they approached Stellwagen Bank, the atmosphere on the boat changed. Strains of Bach wafted over and around the boat. Carol had told them they would pipe music through the PA system because it seemed to attract the whales, and Bach seemed to work the best. Excitement was palpable even as people became more quiet. The captain interrupted the music briefly and in a low voice, just loud enough to be heard, said, "Ladies and gentlemen. Keep your eyes peeled. We might see spouts or even backs of humpbacks. Moby will know they are there before we do. So if you can't see far out to sea, just keep your eyes on the dog. He's never wrong."

Hildy rose and squeezed in to stand right against the railing. The boat was moving very slowly now, not churning the water, and she got a surprise when she looked down. The color of the ocean was a dark slate, almost black, and it looked hard, like if you fell you'd land on it, not in it, and crack your skull. When she thought about it, the lakes back home were not blue either. They were green. Was there any blue water outside people's imaginations? Maybe the Mediterranean? The Caribbean? She didn't care. For now, the captain had stopped the motors and Moby, who had been cadging a bit of bagel from a tourist, suddenly bolted forward and around to the other side of the boat.

"There!" someone cried. "It's a humpback!"

"Please, don't everyone run to the same side of the boat. If they are here, and they are, you'll see them all around."

All but a few people disregarded the captain's request and scurried to the side of the boat where the whale was seen. "There's a calf!" Cameras clicked and people oohed and aahed. Many were silent, witnessing the spectacular, as two humpbacks breached, rising impossibly high, straight up into the air and falling to the side with a sea-displacing splash. The calf, like a curious youngster of any family, swam to the side of the boat, dived under it, and came up on the other side. People were delighted and the calf seemed to enjoy the attention.

Hildy clasped her mittened hands in front of her, so moved she felt near tears. And still, she scanned the waters for any sign of dolphins. She knew they didn't always come around, but sometimes they did. It was not impossible. Moby kept charging around the boat to be on the side where the whale calf emerged, and Hildy hoped he would respond to dolphins in a similar way.

The breaching whales had disappeared, and not long after, the calf swam away and dived. People relaxed a little, the captain announced it was time to turn back, and the lines for more hot coffee and chowder formed in the cabin. Hildy found the bathroom, then went to the concession for more coffee and an egg sandwich. She was pleased to her very core. She felt in her pocket for Marvin's number.

The common lobby/lounge area of the Sea Scape was not used much because most people were out exploring the town, the dunes, and the nightlife, or they were on the boats. So, Hildy spent much of her time there. She could watch her favorite evening television shows, *The Golden Girls* and *Murder, She Wrote* and the news or just sit and read in one of the recliners. But mostly, she enjoyed gazing out the big windows that faced the sea. She couldn't seem to get enough of the view. It was endlessly engaging and it filled her with a contentment she had never known. The staff treated her like their grandmother, bringing her coffee and cookies once in a while, free of charge. They weren't talkative and she appreciated their attentions, which were thoughtful and brief.

Marion and Leona were grown and they were still living with Hildy in her little house a few blocks from Lake Harriet in Minneapolis. Ed came to visit and she said to him, "Why are you here now?" He had only ever taken the girls once every two months or so for an afternoon at the amusement park or the zoo, or in the winter, maybe to a movie. Hildy would have gladly given him joint custody, but he didn't ask for it. Her mother was there too, harping as she always harped about Ed. "Why do you let him into your dreams?" she scolded. "He's always here." "Well, so are you." "Not all the time." Even in her dreams, she knew she was dreaming. By the time Leona was twenty-one and Marion nineteen, Ed was dead. And so was her mother. None of them knew, as she did, that her last thought on this earth would be of Ed Flannigan, even though their marriage had lasted only long enough to produce two in-wedlock children. Neither had married again. Hildy supported them by working in the bank while her mother took care of the girls. Maybe that's why they turned out the way they did. Solid citizens with no imagination. Ed had, well, who knew what this hard drinking, happy-go-lucky Irishman actually did? She knew he was happier than he was lucky, since he always looked down at heel, but clean, sober, and shaved when he came for his daughters. He never remembered their birthdays. They had liked seeing him as they would have a congenial uncle who showed up occasionally, but their feelings didn't run too deep and when he was found dead in a rooming house, they did not mourn.

"Mrs. Flannigan? Mrs. Flannigan?"

"Yes?" She opened her eyes to the smiling face of one of the Sea Scape staff who was lightly touching her shoulder and saying her name.

"They are going to stop serving lunch in half an hour."

"Oh, yes. Thank you." Hildy was a regular for lunch when she wasn't on the boat. She took a moment to clear her head and slowly rose from the recliner where she had spent the last hour, dreaming.

When she planned her trip, Hildy had imagined herself on a whale boat every day, but in the reality she was not up to it. So, she took her mystery novel out to the benches to read and watch the sky and sea. The view was eternal, infinite, and ever changing; her eyes were off her book more than on. She did most of her reading in the evening after her bath in her room.

One day, she called Marvin to take her up Commercial Street so she could wander in and out of the shops. She found a bookstore and was happy to see they had a mystery section, as she was going to come to the end of her Mary Roberts Reinhart paperbacks. She found a coffee shop where she ordered some kind of chocolate-filled pastry and black coffee and perused the local paper. She asked the waitress if it would be possible for the restaurant to call Marvin and have him pick her up outside the shop. They did so and he was there in about ten minutes.

She found that she could only go out on the boat every third day, but she was content with her quiet routine. She always asked the naturalist on board, sometimes it was Carol, sometimes a young man, if they had seen any dolphins. No one had, so she hadn't missed that at least.

After two weeks, which included five whale watches, during which she had seen humpbacks on every occasion, she knew she had to go back home. Provincetown was no longer the sleepy little village it was when she first arrived. The tourist season was picking up and so was the pace. The whale boats were getting crowded and so was the Sea Scape's restaurant. One afternoon there was not a bench free on the lawn for her to sit and read. She asked the concierge to make the calls for her to get reservations home.

She bought one more ticket for a whale watch. She had been on all the boats but one, the Star Dancer, and this morning, she boarded it, noting it was smaller than the others and seemed much older. She found a seat inside at first, as she was accustomed to doing, while she finished her coffee and muffin. She did not go outside until they approached Stellwagon Bank, where today the humpbacks were already spy hopping to the delight of the watchers.

Unlike the other whale boats she had been on, one couldn't walk all the way around the deck of the Star Dancer. The way was obstructed by some metal boxes bolted to the floor. Cables attached to rings at the front of the topmost box stretched to the peaked roof of the captain's glassed-in perch. The obstruction also prevented her taking her favored position, seated facing forward.

She watched the humpbacks now, with a familiarity that pleased her, standing among the first-time whale watchers. Today two small humpbacks, small by whale standards anyway, were putting on quite a show, diving and dancing and circling the boat, or diving beneath it and coming up on the other side. Passengers followed them around and Hildy, keeping her seat as far forward as possible, caught a mercurial glimmer straight ahead of their boat, which was resting still in the water. The flash of silver seemed not to be a whitecap and it was getting closer. She peered hard into the distance. Humpbacks hadn't looked like this when she had seen them and there was no spout. Just silver crescents, yes, more than one, many, peaking above and spearing through the waves. They had to be dolphins. She looked around her. No one else noticed and she glanced up at the captain's perch.

He was looking to his left, at the whales, and Hildy was the only one aware of the smaller moving shapes ahead in the water. She was sure now. They were dolphins. She sat on the side of the box and pulled herself up on her knees, and then to her feet by grabbing one of the cables. She could see better now and made her way forward carefully to the railing so she would be close to them when they approached the boat, as she was sure they must.

Her heart was beating fast and she held her breath and then breathed deeply. She was whispering, "Yes, thank you thank you," to the dolphins, to the sea, to no one in particular. They were leaping closer.

As she leaned out, salt spray carried on the sweet breath of the sea formed droplets like tears on her face. As they reached her lips, she licked them and was back in the last row of the ramshackle movie theatre, a lifetime ago, where that Gish girl silently portrayed all the sorrow and sweetness of a hopeless love, so that Hildy cried and was embarrassed because it was only her second date with Ed Flanagan. She didn't want him to catch her crying. She would feel humiliated if he laughed. She risked a glance at him, hoping he was looking at the screen and hadn't noticed her tears, and something unfolded inside her when she found him glancing shyly at her with tears of his own wetting his cheeks. They came together, hands touching hands and faces lightly, caressingly, kissing softly and licking the tears from each other's faces, like butterflies at roses—a gentle prelude to a rhapsody that sent her that night, not home to her father's house and her own bed, but to Ed's and his. For ten years that passion danced between them like a joyous flame until it died as astonishingly as it was born, leaving a trail of tender ashes. The memory washed over her in less than a heartbeat as she leaned out trying hard to catch every flash of silver, arcing, plunging toward her in the sea. Suddenly she was out of balance and her hand gave up its grip on the cable. She fell forward, toppling over the side into the dark water.

The ocean closed over her at once. Her breath was knocked out of her on impact and the icy cold made her gasp, but she couldn't. Her throat was sealed. There was a searing rip all down her middle, a moment of utter blackness, and then she saw them clearly, swimming toward her—six dolphins, gleaming in the light-drenched water. *Oh, I was so afraid I wouldn't see you!* They laughed and greeted her with one mind, and yet she clearly sensed six distinct individuals. She understood she could be part of that mind too, and still be herself. She was happy.

Come with us, they invited.

She followed them feeling a strength and lightness of being that she remembered from a lifetime ago. *I can swim!*

Of course. They replied. *You can fly, too.*

I can?

You'll see. Their silent, merry laughter flashed silver in her mind as their bodies gleamed in the water.

Oh, look. She had turned back to see several people, two in the water and three on board, struggling to lift out a lumpish, dripping mass. *Oh dear, they should just leave it.*

The dolphins laughed again, their gentle merry laugh that she could feel more than hear. *That sort of thing is important to them. Let's go.*

She swam with them and they frolicked about her on all sides in water that changed from indigo to lightening shades of blue, to silver and then to gold. The waters became richer and warmer with golden light, and then she could see stars and systems of stars.

On board the Star Dancer, the whale watchers and crew were in shock. Those that had dived into the water now shivered inside blankets while others leaned over the lifeless body of the cute little old lady. A woman looked up and out to sea. "Look," she said and pointed. "Dolphins."

I'm never quite sure when he's talking about the grizzly in general, and when he means *the* old bear, the one who maimed him, the one he's been trying to save his whole life, almost.

"Yup, the trouble with Old Bear...he don't negotiate. He's too smart to waste his valuable time negotiatin' with a white man. He knows no white man ever kept a treaty." The old man chuckles. "There I expect he's smarter than the Indian. Now don't you go tellin' Jamesy I said that. (He wags his finger at me sternly. I say, "No, Grandad.") Though I expect Jamesy knows it all right. Nope, the Indians lived 'long side Old Bear for hundreds and hundreds of years." With a sweep of his left arm he takes in the span of years like they are hills stretching out before him in the glow of the setting sun. "I heard some say—though I never seen it—that they know'd Old Bear to kill a sheep and only eat its liver. Leave the rest. Well, hell, I seen white men do the same to a whole herd of buffalo. Seen that myself. Shoot 'em down, cut their tongues out. Just their tongues, mind you, and leave the carcasses to rot. Or skin 'em for them fancy buggy rags back East. Naw, that's nuthin to hate Old Bear for. Nuthin at all. But we hate him. We do."

Grandad loves the bear. He settles back in his chair, squints into the distance, and rubs the stump of arm hanging from a lifeless right shoulder.

My dad and my uncle Joe tell me of the times they've seen the old man stand up against the whole valley, offering to pay out of his own pocket for sheep they said were taken by the bear. Many's the time, they say, Grandad stopped the ranchers from sending out every able-bodied man and boy to hunt the bear down. And the only reason they backed off was not the money, though some of them took it, all right,

Tiger Dreams

LAST NIGHT I DREAMED OF tigers—or maybe only one—smashing through doors and gates and gates. She leapt up the side of my house and hung there, roaring, her claws hooked through the window screen, which gave, and she pulled herself through.

I'm just a breath ahead of her hot roar, her scythe teeth, hammer paws, and claws that will rake places in dreamtime already scarred in real time—a reversing of scare and scar that amuses me, awake, as some profound, unsharable joke.

Tonight, I will let her catch me.

The Old Man and the Bear

The story is stranger in the telling than it was in the living, for at the time, we had Jamesy, and he made everything seem inevitable and natural. Jamesy was Blackfoot: a solitary man and the old man's best friend. It was the bear brought them together—a testament to the fineness of Jamesy's nature that he took in the young white man he found mangled and bleeding to death, since rumor had it that as a boy, Jamesy had watched while soldiers massacred his village. He rarely spoke except to Hiram, and even that was little.

As Hiram recovered, he nursed no ill will toward the bear who had nearly killed him, but listened to the Blackfoot's legends of the grizzly bear. The great bear is ancestor to the Blackfoot people, Jamesy said. He spoke with reverence and called the bear Grandfather.

In remembering, I am there again. I can feel the evening wind blow across the valley and ruffle my wispy hair that always flies loose from the braids that Gramma Ez does for me every morning. I hear the creak of the old man's rocker against the slats of the porch as we sit, supervising the sunset, him telling me Old Bear stories and me asking him the same questions to lead him on. "The trouble with Old Bear," he says, "is he's got attitude."

but because of his scars and the blue fire in his eyes when he faced them.

But there are changes in the valley. The old folks, the ones who remember Hiram Cutter in his prime, are almost all gone, and the younger ones aren't so respectful of an old man's shoulder. Some of them, I hear, even doubt he was ever mauled by a bear, and some of them doubt that it is the same bear that comes down from the mountains once in a while in the spring to eat their sheep. The valley is changing all right. The little town is creeping out over the land. There are more ranches, more fences. You have to ride almost to the foothills now, Dad says, to run out of private property anymore. "Too many people," Grandad grumbles. "Too many. It ain't gonna work, this many people."

"What ain't, Grandad?"

He just looks at me and rubs his mangled arm.

Grandad is full of Old Bear stories. One of his favorites is the time old Jeremiah Jenkins, that's JJ Senior—he's dead now—set a trap for Old Bear in one of his mud wallows down by the creek. "Yup, he set this here big trap and attached it to a log, you know, so he could follow Old Bear through the brush after he was caught and so the bear would be tired out from pullin' and bleedin'. So after a couple days, old JJ Senior goes back to check on his trap, and don't you know..." Grandad stomps the slats with his feet and laughs and laughs, "when he gets back there, he sees that Old Bear has relieved himself smack on his trap. Quite a heap it was, too. Well, that made JJ Senior so disgusted he didn't even try to clean it up. It was a mess! Ooowee! He just left it there to rust out by the creek, sprung by a pile of bear shit!" The old man laughs so hard he's wiping his eyes. I laugh, too. Every time.

But to get out of him my favorite story I just have to ask, "Grandad, why don't you hate Old Bear?"

"Cuz he's a forgivin' bear. He let me off with just..." he looks for the word and finds it as he always does in the back of his memory pile where he stores bits of the sermons he's heard over the years from being coaxed to church every Sunday by Gramma Ez. "He let me off with just a... exhortation. I was young, headstrong, sort of a drifter, you know, and headed for trouble. Full of attitude myself, you see. I stumbled into him like the fool I was, sassed him like the bigger fool I was, and he taught me a lesson. He could of killed me, but he knew what a harmless little grub I was. I didn't have no gun on me or nuthin', nor fat neither, so I wasn't more'n a mouthful, so he give me a tap. A love tap. Yup. A forgivin' bear."

Hiram Cutter is seventy-five, thin, brown, and tough as a hank of jerky, sun dried, wind cured, and salty. Men like Grandad—hardy sheep ranchers and a few old mountain men that still hang onto the mountains like scrub brush, only showing up in town once a year to buy coffee and tobacco—these men never die in their beds. They don't get sick and fade away. They get up, go to work, and drop dead behind the barn, or climbing over the next rise, or calling their dogs, or brushing down their mules. I can't imagine death ever coming to the old man. I see him going up the mountain and turning into a tree or a blackbird or something, and starting life fresh, but never can I see him diminished in any way.

"Don't mistake me, Girl. I ain't no blasphemer, but you know the story of Paul on the road to Damascus. He was struck blind so he could learn somethin'."

"Yeah, Grandad, but Paul recovered, didn't he?"

"That's right, and so did I. Jamesy found me and carried me back to his cabin, that same over the hill there. I lay half dead and mostly crazy for days and nights. But I recovered. This arm you see here missin', why I didn't need it! I've put in a full day's work every day of my life since then, married a good woman, got me two fine sons and one fair-to-middlin' granddaughter (he pulls on my braid). Now I never could of done that with all the attitude I was burdened with as a young buck. Why, Esmeralda wouldn' of give me the time a day while I was in that pitiful condition. Just like we wouldn' of had no religion without Paul learnin' somethin' that day, and it took a stroke to teach him, I'll tell you. Well, Old Bear taught me. He sure did. And I've been a happy man. A man can't ask for more than that."

"No, Grandad."

"Yup, it's going to rain tomorrow. Old Bear tells me so." He rubs his shoulder. The stump of arm left from the Old Bear's swipe is the surest weather report in the valley. Grandad says, "Nope, it's gonna storm tomorrow," and folks run to batten down the hatches. "Frost tonight, Mama. Cover your roses. Old Bear tells me so," and the roses wind up under a pile of straw. Old Bear is never wrong.

The old man liked to work. I can't remember any particular time when it happened, but one day I knew that Grandad was not happy. Dad had been gradually turning the ranch into something bigger over the years. We had several hired hands who lived on the place, and Dad hired extra hands for the lambing and shearing. They were all young and tough, except Pete, who was older than my father but nowhere near as old as Grandad. It seemed the old man was spending more time fussing with the tackle in the barn and tending Gramma Ez's flower beds than he was herding sheep or mending fences or digging wells. He helped at lambing time—we all did—but he was gently being put to pasture, as he told me once. I know my father thought he was doing Grandad a favor. "Dad, take it a little easy. We got plenty of hands now. You don't have to work so hard." But Grandad would grumble and go off to find something to do. Anything at all.

Then came that spring when Old Bear came down out of the mountains and started killing sheep...and didn't stop. The ranchers were all riled up, but nobody could even get a glimpse of the bear, never mind take a shot at him, and Grandad just shook his head. "Something's wrong with Old Bear. He never went on like this before...a few sheep here and there...a dog or two...he's gettin' old, I reckon. Can't cut the mustard. Sheep's an easy meal for an old porker." I think the old man felt for the bear, even when it was our sheep that were found mangled and half-eaten.

Some still doubted that it was the same bear taking sheep as had attacked the old man in his youth. But he knew it was. The bear was old and sheep were handy. Handy...they were all over the place. No more berry patches or honey troves or favored roots...everything was gone to sheep. So, Old Bear ate sheep.

By the end of July, the valley was in a frenzy. They ignored Grandad's offers of money and sheep to repay their losses and tried to track the grizzly. But still, nobody ever saw the bear, they just found the results of his carnage.

A meeting was called to decide whether or not to hire a professional bear hunter. My father had lost sheep too, and he was, I think, inclined to side with those who wanted the grizzly shot, but out of respect for Grandad he didn't come right out and say so. Dad and Grandad went to the meeting. It was held on a Sunday at the town hall and they left on horseback right after dinner, about 1:30.

Ma and Gram and I sat in the kitchen all afternoon and played cards. It was getting dark; Ma had just lit the lamps when we heard their horses. They went right to the barn. It takes a little while to unsaddle and tend to a horse properly, so Ma and Gramma took their time fixing sandwiches and coffee. I went out on the porch to wait. I waited. And waited. Through the window I could see the table set and Ma sitting down sipping her coffee and Gramma working on her crocheting. Finally, Dad came out of the barn. He looked...different. He put his hand on my head as he passed me but didn't say anything. I followed him into the kitchen. In the light of the kerosene lamps I could see why my father looked the way he did. He'd been crying. It was a shock because I'd never seen a man cry. I didn't think they could. Gram just looked at him and rested her crocheting in her lap. Ma looked scared. "John? What happened?"

"They'd already made their minds up to it. They already had the guy's name and where to telegraph him—the bear hunter. But they took a vote. Dad and I didn't vote. It was unanimous. Then Dad got up and he said since their minds was made up, he'd have no hired killer take the Old Bear." My father's voice broke. "He's going after him himself." He took off his hat and ran his fingers through his hair and put his hat back on. Dad never wore his hat in the house. Gramma Ez was quiet, and Ma said, "You're not going to let him?" My father shouted at her. He'd never done that before, either. Dad never shouted at anybody. But he was shouting now. "What am I going to do, lock him up in the barn? What do you want me to do?"

"We have to do something," Ma said in a small voice.

"We'll give him these sandwiches. He'll be getting hungry, I expect." That was Gramma Ez putting aside her yarn-work and starting to wrap up the sandwiches they had made for our supper. She put them in a bag and handed them to Dad who was taking the gun off the rack. As he was going out the door, he turned to me and said, "Abby, as soon as I'm in the barn—make sure Grandad don't see you—run and get Jamesy."

"Yes, Daddy."

I watched him cross the yard in long strides. His back was stooped. He'd never looked small to me before. As soon as he closed the barn door behind him, I took off behind the house and headed up over the hill, past the graveyard where Gramma Ez's people were buried. Jamesy's cabin was "just over the hill" but it was at least three miles—five if you took the road, but I didn't. I ran all the way. His Indian ears heard me coming even though I thought I was pretty quiet. Jamesy was standing on his porch, waiting for me. I was gulping air but managed to spit out the gist of what was happening back at our place.

"Wait," he said. He went to his little barn and led out his pony. He still rode the Indian way, with no saddle. Jamesy was about the same age as Grandad, I guess, but it was hard to tell. He'd always looked the same. His face was so lined and brown it looked like tree bark. His hair was long and mostly black still. He tied it with a piece of leather, and it hung down his back like a tail. He reached down and hauled me up behind him. He smelled of wood smoke and sheep—kind of a good smell—and I put my arms around him, waiting for the gallop. He walked the pony all the way. "Jamesy, don't you think we should run?" He said, "No."

Jamesy didn't go after the old man, who, of course, was long gone by the time we got back. I had assumed that was what Dad wanted him to do. Jamesy would have been the only one who could follow Grandad without his knowing it. And maybe I was right, because Dad looked stricken to see us ambling into the yard the way we were doing, with no sense of urgency apparent.

Jamesy so seldom spoke, that when he did, it was a matter of notice. Even in the dark, he could see my father's face as he came down the porch steps to greet us and lift me down from the pony, and he said in a voice that sounded younger than his face (I guessed because he didn't use it much, it didn't age with the rest of him), "John, let's bed down the pony. Come to the barn." I'd never heard him put so many words together in one string. My father didn't say a word. He just went to the barn with Jamesy. They were there about thirty minutes. What Jamesy told him, I don't know. Dad never did say.

Ma made me go to bed early. When I woke up, Jamesy was sitting on our porch with a cup of coffee in his hand looking out on the horizon. That day, the hired men did the work and my father made a show of working, but he stayed close to the house. Jeremy Jenkins—JJ Junior—came over and seemed to be inquiring for the rest of the valley. At least he gave himself airs as a spokesman. What was going on? Was the old man to be trusted? Could he kill the bear? Could he even find the bear?

Dad lost his temper and for the second time I heard him yell. He told JJ Junior that they had, every one of them, agreed to let Grandad try. If *he* couldn't track the bear, nobody could, and they had demonstrated *that* all summer long, and if Grandad said he was going to do something, he'd do it by God, his word was as good as any man's, and he almost threw JJ Junior bodily off the place. Pete had to step in to keep him from taking a punch at JJ Junior. After that, Pete stayed pretty close to my father, and there were no more visitors of an inquiring mind.

Jamesy stayed on with us, and by that time, my uncle Joe was there too. Jamesy was the glue that held us together, though I couldn't see why and nobody said so, but I felt it was true. If Jamesy hadn't been there, Lord alone knows what might have happened. He sort of kept the lid on things, just sitting on the porch, sipping Ma's coffee, waiting. He wasn't wasting time. He knew what he was waiting for, even if the rest of us didn't. Gramma Ez was quiet, too. *Inside* quiet, I mean. Everybody talked less than usual, but only Gram and Jamesy were kind of peaceful, watchful and peaceful. Gramma moved her rocker to the porch on one side of the door; Jamesy was in a chair on the other side. He was just looking and waiting; she was rocking and crocheting. Ma cooked and cleaned like her life depended on it. Maybe it did. She cleaned the house so much she nearly rubbed it away. We had more food laid on than anybody could possibly eat, especially since nobody was really hungry except the hands who did manage to put it all away.

After four terrible days, Jamesy, hearing some cue nobody else heard, told Pete to saddle up his strongest horse and come with him. He wouldn't let Dad or Joe go along.

We waited all day. Ma and Gramma kept busy, Dad and Joe took over the chairs on the porch and gave up all pretense of working. Dark came on and the lamps were lit. Ma kept the coffee going but finally gave up the cooking. Nobody made me go to bed. I think they forgot all about me and I kept quiet. We waited all night. As the light from the lamps got lost in the dawn, my father blew them out and we followed him onto the porch to wait there. We were all out there: Ma and Gramma, Daddy and Joe, me, and Pete's wife, Shirley. We all saw them at once, I think, as they came over the rise down the trail to the ranch. Jamesy and Pete were walking, leading three horses. As they plodded into focus we made out that the horses were hitched in tandem to a large travois bearing a double burden. Jamesy had brought back, not just the body of my grandfather, but that of Old Bear as well. For the second time I saw my father cry. Joe cried, too. And Ma.

Dad and Joe went out to meet them. Pete seemed to do most of the talking. Dad and Joe just listened. Then Jamesy said something and Dad and Joe nodded their heads. Joe went with Jamesy and the horses and travois, and Dad brought Pete back to the house. "Tell 'em, Pete," he said. Ma had her arm around Gramma. So did Shirley, but Gramma Ez looked better than they did. I guess she knew the old man better than any of them and was more prepared. Pete took off his hat and ran a meaty hand back and forth across his bald head. "I don't know, John…like I was sayin', ma'am, (that was to Gramma Ez) this was just the damnedest thing I ever seen. We found Hiram's horse first, wandering toward home. The rifle still strapped to the saddle. So it looks like he just walked up to the old bear and stuck his knife in him. The bear took a swipe at him all right. His chest is laid open some, but not bad. Not like I've seen. I've seen a bear turn a man inside out, but this was a clean swipe. Clean and deep enough, so the old man bled to death...but he didn't exactly die of the wound, you understand. The wound could have been fixed up okay, I think. And the bear...well, I don't know. I've seen grizzlies walk away full of bullets and knife wounds a whole hell of a lot worse than this one the old man gave him. So I don't know. We found 'em, they was both lying on the ground dead, the old man wrapped in the bear's hug, so I thought he must have been crushed, you know, by the bear's grip. But nothing was broken. No ribs, nothing. Jamesy and I both checked. They was both a little warm still when we got there. It was...just the damnedest thing. There was no sign of fightin'...no signs of struggle. Nuthin. The horse wasn't even skittish when we found her. She was just wanderin' around grazing, making her way home, like I said. It seemed like they just laid down and let themselves bleed to death. Like the two of 'em, I don't know, like they decided on something. Just the damnedest thing." Pete kept rubbing his bald head, then finally replaced his hat. "I'm sorry, ma'am. I better go and help Jamesy. We're going to bury him now, if you don't mind, ma'am."

Then Dad said to Gramma Ez, "Ma, do you want to see him? He's not injured bad, just covered with bear blood mostly. But he looks like he's sleepin'..." and then my father went all to pieces, sobbing like he just couldn't get to the bottom of how bad he felt, and Gramma put her thin arms around him like he was a little boy again and just crooned, "There, John, I'm sorry, John."

So that afternoon they buried my grandad in the family burial ground on the hill behind the house, and Jamesy set a fire around the bear a little way from the old man's grave. I think he would have liked to bury Grandad the Indian way, you know, not bury him at all but put him up on poles, closer to heaven, the way they do, but he knew it wasn't our way, so he just helped dig the grave and put Grandad in it. But he built his fire around the huge carcass of the bear. And we listened to him all day and all that night, softly chanting in his own language. It was eerie, but comforting in a way, too. Gramma Ez went out on the porch and sat, I think so she could listen better. He sat on the hill cocooned in his blanket for a day or two—I don't remember—chanting for the old man and for the bear. Ma made food for me to take to him, but he would take only water. He chanted till the fire burned out. Then he scattered the ashes all over, took his pony, and went home.

It took a little while for the valley to find out that the bear and Grandad were both dead. After a few days the minister came out and said some words over the grave, and if he noticed the huge charred spot where something had been burned recently, he didn't comment. I suppose he and most of the valley would have been outraged at Jamesy's heathen ritual, but all of us, even the hands, kept our mouths shut. And if the rumors flew, as I'm sure they did, they never got back to us. Anyway, we knew what Jamesy did was what the old man, and maybe even the bear, would have liked.

The Subway Mouse

SHE LIVES IN THUNDER, FORAGING in meadows of steel and concrete amid slimy pools, sources unspeakable, she ekes a living from human garbage. And still she lives and wants to live.

Steel bites steel and spits fire over the place her soft body was a heartbeat ago, before she disappeared beneath the rail into a dank world far from sun and air and fragrant rooty earth. And still she lives and wants to live.

The Ballad of the Sad Young Man

(Based on a true story, as told by a former orca
trainer to a meeting of the NY/NJ Chapter
of the American Cetacean Society)

I WAS OUT OF A job, at loose ends, and had time to kill,
so I went to see the show. Dolphins flying through hoops in
rhythm and sync. Rainbowed splashes. Children squealing.
Handclaps and tail flips and a trainer with a mike in his hand:
"Thank you. Thank you very much, and Flipper thanks you,
too." Paper wrappers snapping. People munching peanuts
and popcorn and sucking caramel off their teeth. Sun hats
adjusted. Sunglasses pushed up sweaty noses. A murmur
like a wave wells through the crowd. Then the silence of
anticipation. "Ladies and gentlemen: ORCA! THE KILLER
WHALE!" A gate melts into the water; a giant shape—
ebony and alabaster—glides over it soundlessly, dives deep
and leaps gleaming, pure in his whiteness, absolute in his
blackness, a yin yang of no-color and form. The spectators,
awed, cannot clap at once. Rose-cheeked children stare,
mouths agape, eyes wide and fearless.

After the show, I made my way backstage and asked for a
job, certain they would turn me down. I had no experience.
Could I swim? Yes. They hired me. On the spot. Because

the trainer, who was no trainer but an out-of-work-actor who would do anything to be in front of a crowd with a mike in his hand, wanted to take his tan to New York but couldn't because of his contract. I made it possible for him to break and run. So, there I was, an orca trainer. "Don't worry. You'll learn the routine. Nothing to it," the actor said. "Watch him, though." He pointed to the orca whose sharp dorsal fin sliced the water as he swam broodingly round and round his holding tank. I walked over to have a closer look, and Orca looked at me, and I felt his gaze like a jolt of electricity down through my guts to the soles of my feet and up again right out the top of my skull and tears came—from where?—to my eyes, for I had not been prepared for this and I will never be the same again.

It wasn't part of my job, but I spent as many hours with Orca as I could, because he was captive and alone and I couldn't help him except to keep him company. Every evening I went to his tank to say good night. Once, as I was leaving him, I turned and saw him watching me, one great unfathomable eye framed in the glass window of the tank—watching me as I walked away. Free.

Most mornings were given to training the dolphins and general maintenance of the performance pool. Audiences were not allowed in until 1:30 for the afternoon shows. On this morning, I was watching Orca swimming quietly in the performance pool where I left him as long as I could every day, because it was roomier than his holding tank. We had just finished our play session. (We never trained—there was nothing I could teach Orca. He made up new routines to relieve his boredom, and I had only to be sharp enough to catch on to them.) Enter my least favorite colleague: a cocky young man in love with commanding cetaceans.

The dolphins didn't seem to mind him, but Orca didn't like him, and the man especially didn't like Orca.

In a hurry to get through his training session with the dolphins, he jogged out onto the high diving board that extended over the performance pool to regale us all with directions of opening the gate to the orca tank and bringing the dolphins in pronto. The board was slick. He was careless. He slipped and fell feet first into the pool. With cetacean prescience, or perhaps just hopefulness, Orca was poised at the bottom of the pool—just below the diving board.

In the time it took for the dolphin trainer to feel the jaws closing upon him underwater and holding him there, to the moment he felt himself finally lifted into the air, breathing at last but still immobilized, it was obvious that he had acquired the incontrovertible knowledge that Orca held his life in his will; that nothing he could do, and nothing any of us, the trainers, divers, and caretakers who looked on, could do, could save him; that one hairsbreadth miscalculation of a muscle in leviathan's jaws and his ribs would crack like a finch's egg; that he was human and it was humans who held Orca prisoner, made him perform mindless tricks for bits of fish in front of a race of popcorn munchers; stole his dignity and his freedom—he, who had been king of the oceans.

And Orca let him go.

As the dolphin trainer, without even a bruise, scrambled, pale and breathless, out of the water, it was as if we were surrounded by shards of crystal suspended in the air, luminous and tingling. *I can destroy you, but I do not. Because I am an ethical being.* We knew in that shimmery clangor of revelation that we stood in the presence of one with the mind to comprehend his awful and endless predicament and the grace to live without revenge.

I tried everything I could to alleviate Orca's loneliness and boredom, but I was a pathetic substitute for the open seas and the fellowship of his own kind. I tried to justify working for the marina by rationalizing that I cared for Orca and that I was helping to educate others even if I couldn't save Orca himself. This last myth was dispelled the day a man came backstage after a show wanting to inspect the device that animated our model killer whale. Even after I introduced Orca, the man would not believe he was not seeing some clever, lifelike model akin to "Bruce" the mechanical shark used in the movie *Jaws*. He stalked away, angry that we were so uncooperative. I wondered, too, what kind of education we were giving children. "Come see the creatures who have no rights of their own, else how are we justified in keeping them captives for your pleasure?" This wasn't the kind of "education" I could be part of any longer.

Night after night, I ached and tried to explain to Orca and to myself why I couldn't stay and watch him die in captivity while I had no resources to free him.

I work now with free dolphins. I wait hours in the sun for them to appear, and I swim with them when they let me. At night, I sit and gaze at the stars. I think of Orca and feel his eyes still following me.

The Eye of the Whale

(For Paul Watson and the Sea Shepherd warriors)

I LOOKED INTO THE EYE of the whale and saw the person looking back at me, and she said to me, "You are witness. You cannot now turn away," nor could I.

Cords of light, cords of steel bind me to her for all time, and wherever I am, and wherever she is, they are my burden.

They are my joy.

Singers in the Storm

A Meditation on the Flood

It BEGAN WITH A WIND murmuring in an ancient and new voice; the sea nations heard, and only one man, who told his wife. She said, "Ah, you're drunk again." His sons thought the same. Their wives said nothing and listened. Then, they, too, heard the voice of the wind, and gathering close their garments, grew quieter still. They carried cool water to their father-in-law as he, in obedience to the voice, hauled rough-cut planks of cedar—hard labor for a six-hundred-year-old man.

His sons watched their wives and then began to help their father. The old man's wife never heard the voice; nevertheless, she cooked, washed, mended their clothing, and dreamed of grandchildren.

Poised in twilight, she quivers from nose to tail. He steps out of the blackness of the trees. Utterly still, they fathom each other and the wind. Delicate, polished black adamantine hooves tamp ground. With gracile limbs powered by iron-sprung haunches and chests deep and wide for drinking the wind, they leap together into the wind tide, eastward—the stag and his mate.

The wind furrows the backs of the pack lounging outside their den, digesting their kill and watching pups stalk and maul each other. It is not the alpha wolf who rises, shakes himself, pricks his ears, and begins to lope east, moon rising in his eyes, but a young dog a year before his prime. The sloe-eyed she-wolf running northeast converges with him. Matching strides, they cover ground their huge feet seem not to touch, running swiftly for days on end, without rest, without weariness, as if borne by the wind.

The matriarch weeps and flings her head from side to side, swaying and stamping in grief. Caressed by her sister, she will not be comforted. A wind has swept over them at the watering place. The young one lifts her trunk to read it and closes her eyes. Helpless to affect some terrible thing she knows is coming, the matriarch watches her daughter leave the family, trotting into the wind. (The bull sees her coming, tiny by his measure; his eyes fill with tears.)

Gold, with green eyes, she waits. He approaches. Among twigs and leaves, across vines and loose stones, huge feline paws land and break nothing, disturb nothing, make no sound—a silent step he can maintain at all but his top speed. He moves, shadow among shadows, knowing she is there. A growl, begun by instinct, surges from his belly. He ignores it. She, who, before the wind, would have feared him, now whirls and without caution begins to run. He is a loner, but he will go with her. They have been chosen.

Thus, the wind—the wind of doom, the reckoning wind, wind of the Lord's own sorrow—sweeps the earth, Destroyer and Preserver; for as it summons the clouds and churns the waters, it chooses some to cipher its message. Antennae throb, whiskers maneuver, tails twitch, and sticky red tongues snap out to taste. Guard hairs stand erect, muscles tighten and release in speed or lumbering strength, in stealth or ground-close scurrying, each according to his nature, each according to her kind. From dens and aeries, balmy plains and the murky depths of jungle and swamp; from blazoned snow lands, dappled forest worlds, and shadowless deserts, they come. Answering the wind; each in his own way, each in her own time, they come.

The old man stands at the threshold of the ark. In spite of the heat, chills finger his spine. His knees shake and his eyes stream. (He is always maudlin in his cups, but he's had nothing to drink for weeks.) He built the ark in obedience, on faith, not knowing for whom he was building it. Now he knows it was for them—and seeing them—in their numbers, in their unbearable humility, in their strength and fragility—he weeps.

The first to arrive are the birds, alighting on the roof— from tiny brown birds, so plain they disappear against the rough wood, to birds of such bright plumage they stop his breath, he has never seen such glory. Such ones exist in the world! He hadn't dreamed.

They come without fear, two by two. The horizon flows rivers of beings: multitudinous forms, shaggy and sleek, scaled and smooth.

They come hopping on twos, prancing on fours; feet padded, flippered, clawed, webbed, hooved; or they slither on none.

They come, shells on their backs, pouches on their fronts, horns on their heads or protruding out their mouths;

in colors of rainbows and of old leaves. The clowns. The majestics.

They come, eyes like moons or setting suns, like mossy pools sunlit from below, like fire-lit ice or haunted brown of unknown depths.

They come with fingers and toes, grasping tails and old-man-like faces, scampering up the ramp like wizened children.

Lizards of a size that could only have been spawned from his most drunken nightmare steadfastly plod up the gangplank.

Tiny, many-eyed, many-legged creatures float by or cling to the backs and heads and tails of larger folk, possibly unfelt by them. (There he sees a spider with her mate—he fat and sleepy, looking forward to her spinning them a silver traveling berth; she deigning not to eat him for the present.)

They come, fantastic, beloved of God. The old man quakes at his responsibility and craves a drink.

For days and nights they come, and the old man's sons take turns holding him up as he greets each one who enters the ark. Finally, the last two arrive: a small white dog and a small brown one. The old man does not know which is he and which she.

The clouds boil white froth that congeals into a black tide and rolls from earth's edge to earth's edge. Light and color drown in a sea of black. Lightning screeches through the heavens like pain; the earth roars in anguish as she opens. Her fountains gush from the deep.

Father and sons close the ark, huddle in the lower deck and listen to the wrath of God. The boat trembles and bravely stands the scathing wind wielding the sword of purgation—water: sustainer of all life, now become destroyer. The ark shudders as if to break apart as the ground is lost, and the old man prays, *Please let this thing float.* It does. Still he cannot rest. He thinks he hears the wailing of all mankind. He weeps bitterly and covers his head and cannot hear the singing and does not notice the silence of the animals both inside and outside the ark.

His daughters-in-law quietly roam the vessel stroking soft noses, scratching ears, filling troughs, mangers, and bowls. The small, hairy creatures with their old-man faces embrace them, play with their earrings, steal their bangles, chatter, and make them laugh. The two little dogs trot after them, fearing no one, not even the old bull elephant (wisdom having its place in the ark along with fecundity), the resident giant, even beside the mammoth female (of whom he is greatly solicitous for she misses her mother), for he is good and always looks before he steps. The birds of every kind, each with his own song, fill the decks with music. The cats lap milk and purr and lick themselves all over until they gleam in the torch-lit hold. The wolves and bears munch heavy cakes made with every kind of grain and oil and herb, lick each other and doze in beds of straw. The cows, ewes, and she-goats mother the voyagers with their milk and chew their grasses in the shadows of proud bulls and rams. Creeping things spin themselves into pods and dangle from the rafters.

After forty days and nights the wailing ceases, wind and rain withdraw; the singing subsides. The ark comes to rest on still water. The old man uncovers his head. He opens a window and peers out. Everywhere is water and nothing,

nothing else. The young women climb to the outside deck, breathe hungrily, loosen their hair, and bare their arms to the sun, scanning the watery world for the singers. What kind of beings are they? Angels? They must, of course, be angels. Will they show themselves?

Now they see a blackness shadowing swift and strong from the depths of the sea. They hear a mighty rumble and *swoosh!* as the waters part. Before them rises Leviathan— first of creation. She cleaves the water—an impossible ascent from liquid to air, the only solid thing, herself, whirling and falling on her side in a sea-displacing splash. Her hieroglyphic flukes smack the surface as she dives. In the distance, two more such ones of a size they can scarcely comprehend, never having seen mountains at play.

The women have no fear. As if to reassure them anyway, the little shepherds of the sea appear, dancing around the boat. The women begin to clap and dance. Their men join in. Even the old man's wife stares in awe at the smiling behemoths and the small ones frolicking about their tiny ark in the great vastness of the spangled waters. The survivors of God's anger behold the beings who flourish beneath the waves, and wonder. And feel at peace.

For the sea nations had not suffered the Lord's regret. They gleamed like shining lights in God's eyes. The small ones asked, in pity for their earthbound brothers and sisters, that they might, with dolphin mind and agile corporeal forms, encompass and surround them to ease their passage. This the Lord allowed. The giants of the sea, too, felt compassion for the creatures of land, for the terror that was theirs to come. *What can we do?* they prayed. *We are so large, we will add to their terror if they see us coming at them through the waves. The little ones among them won't even be able to see us as we are. We will be to them like walls, like mountains, like dark moons. Give us a means to comfort them.*

The Lord heard their prayer and gifted them with song. And when the rains came they began to sing and filled the earth and skies and waters with their songs, and the animals stopped scrambling in fear and listened and were comforted and waited as the waters rose. The spheres resounded with song from the little blue planet for an awesome thing was happening there. And as the waters rose the shepherds came—the dolphins—leaping and laughing, beaming serenity to guide them in joy and peace; compassion filled the stormy seas as they surrounded dying creatures with love, easing them into the next world.

Be not afraid. Nothing dies. All is spirit. All is reborn. Be at peace.

But men fought each other for higher ground, lost their senses, wailing and cursing, so they could not hear the whales singing them hope and comfort, nor feel dolphin mind ready to guide them safely from the disappearing earth to the infinite realm of light and spirit. Drowned in the maelstrom of their own lamentations, mankind passed over into darkness in needless anguish and wandered till their rage was spent and their fear dissolved. It took a long time for them to find their way to the light.

The ark floats on. The whales sing now to comfort the survivors who sometimes howl in anguish over lost tribes or trumpet in grief for memories of wrinkled faces and loving eyes or pace, restless for a territory to study and conquer. The old man says his prayers morning and evening and fondles the seeds in his pocket that hold the promise of new vines. His wife soothes him and keeps a close eye on the bellies of her daughters-in-law. His sons repair the boat. The young women nurture and are nurtured by the creatures on the ark. Mother Wind rises again and rocks the ark like a cradle. The sky stays bright, the sun hot. The waters recede.

The birds leave first.

The sea of water turned to a sea of mud and none but the birds could go far, but the wind sucked the mud dry, and the earth became firm and even green, and the rainbow appeared, sign of the covenant He had made, the Lord God, with the race of men and the beings, every one, he had saved on the ark. And to the minds in the waters who had served the earth's creatures in their dying hours, the Lord God said You will save and shepherd mankind and sing for the peace of all living things. This is your covenant, first of my children. But you will pay dearly, for the riders of the ark have inherited corruption. You will have to sing them back again and again.

The singing hasn't stopped.

The Devil's Due

SAINT PETER ASKS EACH ONE applying at the gates of heaven, *Did you ever beat a horse?* If the answer is "yes," no further questions, the devil take him. *Next!*

If the answer is "no," Saint Peter checks the balance of the person's life. If evil outweighs the good, the saint asks, *Did you ever give water to a thirsty horse? Did you ever ease his burden? Shelter him? Salve his wounds? Or keep him from fear?*

If the answer is "no," the balance remains weighted in the devil's favor. Saint Peter, quite sadly, shakes his head. *Next!*

If the answer is "yes" to any of the questions, Saint Peter sweeps the dross from the devil's side of the balance and leads the person into Paradise, which is full of horses.

Two Photographs Taken
Outside Gubbio

Haggard wolf eye
sees him coming – a
small man, ragged
barefoot, empty
handed.
I will eat him.

More lonely than
ravenous, the
wolf leans
into the open
hand,
weeping.

NON-FICTION

Trixie

A KITTEN FOUND MY GRANDMOTHER. The year was about
1915. Will and Lena Magnus took a rare night out to the only
entertainment in a stark prairie town, a silent flickering
movie, shown in a drafty, unheated hall above the old bank.
People sat bundled inside their coats and mufflers, their
caps pulled down over their ears. My grandmother kept her
hands deep in the muff on her lap.

Throughout her whole long life, my grandma was
squeamish about things that wiggled, crawled, squirmed,
or scampered, and she was especially prone to hysterics
if some hapless small creature surprised her. I remember
her, even when she was quite elderly, running down our
driveway, her arms in the air, her apron flying, crying,
"Ayee!! Ayee!! Ayeee!!!" in her automatic flight response
at the sudden appearance of a tiny lizard in the bathtub.
(It wasn't even a real lizard. My father had placed a rubber
lizard in her tub as a prank.)

She was also the original cat person. She loved cats.
She understood them. She communed with them. In one of
the last photos of her, taken in her nineties, she is holding
a cat, a black-and-white stray someone had given her. They
are cheek-by-whiskers, and both look like they are smiling.

But back to that icy movie theatre in 1915: there is my young grandmother, not even a mother yet, sitting in the cold and dark, watching flickering black-and-white figures chase each other on the screen, and something small and furry and warm crawls inside her muff.

Why she did not rise out of her chair with an "Ayee!!!" and fly out of the theatre in panic has remained a mystery to me, but she didn't. She always said, "You see, I knew it was a kitten."

"But, Grandma, it could have been a mouse or a rat. A skunk! It could have been a weasel or even a badger!" Even as a child, I was given to hyperbole.

"No," she would answer with deep assurance, "I knew it was a little cat. It crawled into my muff and I kept still. It was just a little bit of a thing, mind you. It was cold, don't you see? It crawled in there to keep warm and fell right to sleep. I didn't say anything to Will. I just carried the muff home and put it on the bed, and sure enough, when the little cat woke up, she crawled out of the muff and sat on the bed just as nice as you please looking up at me. Was Will ever surprised! He said, 'You're not going to keep it, are you?' and I answered him right back, 'You're blame tootin' I am.' I fed her. She lapped up a dish of cream with a little bread in it and went right back to sleep. I named her Trixie. I always like the name Trixie for a cat. She grew up so nice and big, and she was like a dog in some ways, you know—never let any other cats or dogs either into our yard. She had gold eyes and a brown nose, sort of a chestnut color I guess you could say. I did think her ears were awfully big, though, but Oh! was she pretty! She had fur that was kind of gold with dark brown stripes running all through it. She was pretty! And from that little bit of a thing in my muff she grew up so nice and big."

Then there was the time old Doc Peabody came over for coffee. Doc Peabody was one of the few people in town who had an education—had seen something of the world, so to speak. He sat in Lena's tiny, immaculate kitchen, sipping his black coffee with sugar, and Trixie, grown by that time, walked through the door in her full majesty, padded across the floor in front of him, and sat at my grandmother's feet. Doc Peabody spilled his coffee all over his suit. "My God!"

Lena, a young, rosy, fresh housewife in a white starched apron, said, "What's the matter?" fearing he was having a stroke or something.

Doc Peabody, seeing Trixie waiting politely by the sink, and apparently realizing she was no hallucination, regained some of his composure. "Where'd you get the bobcat?" he asked.

Grandma told me, "'Bobcat,' I said. Well, I didn't know she was a bobcat. I'd never seen one before and he said, 'Yes, that's a bobcat you've got there. Did you ever see a house cat get that big?' Well, I never thought about it, you see, she was just a little bit of a thing when I found her. 'What are you going to do with it?' he asked me. And I said, 'Well, right now, I am going to give her a saucer of milk.' And that made him stop and think. He never said another word. And he didn't come over for coffee for a long time, either."

Trixie was a watch cat and a guard cat. She kept a careful eye on everything, especially my grandmother. No one approached without first being subject to the cat's penetrating and disconcerting golden stare. "I always felt safe when Trixie was here," Grandma said.

Trixie lived with my grandmother for many years, and when the bobcat died, she left a hole in my grandmother's life that was never filled by another animal, nor, I suspect, by a human.

She told the story often, "She was just a little bit of a thing, mind you..."

Facing the Cat

SHEEPDUNG IS A ZEN-LIKE RESORT in the mountainous area not far from Mendocino, California. Each cottage is unique and spare, designed with just enough accoutrements to be perfectly comfortable but not fancy.

I had never been in such an isolated place before and I was nervous, what with the warning on their website running in a loop in my mind. "What to do if you meet a mountain lion." Well, honeys, if you *see* a mountain lion, it's too dang late. I've *read books* on mountain lions and I know they will stalk you and eat you. Put me down in a pack of wolves; I'll sleep like a baby. Place me in the path of a black bear and I know I have better than a 95 percent chance of snapping a picture and walking away. But mountain lions are not gourmets. If it's warm and moving, they'll eat it. Even if it's not moving. They are one of the few North American land mammals (the grizzly and the polar bear are the other two) to have not one qualm about dining on humans.

One of the owners of Sheepdung told me he had never seen a mountain lion. "Good for you," I said. Behind Tree House, the highest, farthest, most inaccessible cabin, *my* cabin, is a 4' x 3' mound. I know in my heart it is the grave of a half-eaten tourist.

Also behind and above Tree House is a hiking trail, referred to as Cardiac Trail by those who have climbed it, because it is so steep. Well, since I was mortally afraid to do it, I decided I'd better climb it. So, I huffed and I puffed for several hours, and I made it up, not all the way, of course, but a good part of the way, keeping my eyes peeled and my ears cocked for large predators. The largest creature I encountered was a grasshopper. Don't underestimate those little buggers! They jump and *thwhap!* against one's bare leg and it stings like blazes. But I digress. I got far enough UP so that when I finally turned around—if that were to have been my last view of the earth, it would have been worth it.

I'm enjoying the view, getting my wind, and then I realize that the only way back down is BACK DOWN.

That was a lot trickier. Steep. But I managed to keep my footing and not slide down on my butt, as I was afraid I'd have to, which, in jeans, would not have been so bad, but like a dumb tourist, I had made the climb in my QVC polyester shorts.

I did see two paw prints, solidified in the trail, which at one time (how long ago did they have rain?) was mud. They were not big enough for a full-grown cat—the stride wasn't long enough either; maybe a juvenile or a bobcat. I don't know what other wild things roam there. It was way too big for a dog and anyway, I know the difference between a canine and a feline print.

So, I made it down the mountain to my cabin, my haven— NOT. It was a structure made of thin wood and glass...one swipe of a mighty paw, hell—one exhalation of the big bad cat, and the thing would come down. I determined the best course of action in case of feline attack would be to get into the shower. It was at least heavy-gauge molded Plexiglas.

In retrospect, I see now that it was probably my QVC shorts that saved me. Mountain lions may not be gourmets, but they draw the line at polyester.

Seery

SHE WASN'T MY CAT.

My first night in New York—it was two o'clock in the morning. I had just moved in that day and had tried to get everything unpacked all at once. I had almost succeeded and was exhausted.

Then I heard the meowing. "Oh, no!" I aimed my flashlight out my window. All I could make out was barbed wire, chain-link fence, and a courtyard full of junk. By the sound, I was afraid a cat might be caught in something out there. If my little high-powered beam did land on a cat stuck, what could I do at this hour anyway? I had no access to the back of my building. The door into the courtyard from my building was in the basement; the door to the basement was barred and locked as if the nation's gold were stored down there. As far as I knew, it was only the garbage. As I am on the main floor, there are bars on my windows, and the courtyard is completely enclosed. I would have to find someone, in some building over the weekend with keys, who would be willing to let me, a complete stranger, poke around back there. At any rate, if I did discover a cat tangled up, I would have a very hard time rescuing it.

Finally, the meowing stopped and I went to bed. The next night, about the same unearthly hour, meowling began again, closer. I directed my flashlight beam out into the night. There on the raised cement walkway, behind the fence, was a cat, looking at me. The green of her eyes reflected my light like a backlit sea in some mythical kingdom. She was not caught in anything. In fact, she pranced back and forth a couple of times and sat again to stare at me. She seemed to say with her manner and with those incredible eyes, "I just wanted to get your attention."

"You little rat!" I scolded. "Now you let me sleep!" I went back to bed. She was quiet the rest of that night.

The next night there was no meowing. I woke up—unusual for me—at dawn, when my poorly windowed apartment was not pitch black but gray, dim as a bunker in a brownout. The green-eyed cat was sitting on my oak table, quietly gazing at me. How long she had been there, I had no idea. Nothing was disturbed. She had simply walked in through my window (the bars are widely enough spaced for a cat, not for a human) and settled herself on my table. I decided I'd better buy a screen for that window and nudged my poodle, sleeping at the foot of my bed, "Some watchdog." She yawned and rolled over.

I got up and addressed the cat, "Listen you, go back out the way you came in." She obliged by gracefully leaping to the windowsill, trilling her farewell, and scrambling down the side of my building and up the cement wall opposite to the raised courtyard beyond, where she slipped through a space in the chain-link fence.

She appeared to be in good condition. A neighbor said he thought she belonged to someone in a building across the courtyard. I did not approve of cats being allowed to wander like this in the heart of New York City, but she seemed to be thriving, she wasn't my cat, and I didn't know how to find the owners.

Other cats came to my window who were obviously strays. I fed them and the gray tiger with the mystical green eyes defended her territory around my window fiercely. I had to throw food quite a distance for these poor little waifs to get their share. One of these cats finally jumped up to my windowsill and I took him straight to the vet and eventually found him a honeypot of a home. But that is another story. Most came for a night and were gone, never to be seen again. But the gray tiger with sea-green eyes came every day, usually about the time I got home from work, and again around nine o'clock in the evening.

She talked to me in the way cats do, and I talked back. She liked me to pet her and scratch her behind her ears, but she wouldn't allow me to pick her up. Her visits were pleasant. I have been cursed with a severe allergy to cats. I can never live with a cat. The cats I've rescued have gone straight to veterinarians and then to foster or permanent homes. I can keep them in my bathroom for only a few hours, because even with the door closed, I soon become quite ill. So, this was an ideal situation; I was visited daily, sometimes twice a day, by this lovely cat. She announced herself with a forceful meow "I'm here!" and then lingered on my windowsill, trilling in a soft conversational way.

Her green eyes often met mine as an equal. She came for friendship, not for a handout. This pleasant friendship went on for nearly two years.

I went on vacation for two weeks. A friend planned to stay in my apartment for a week while I was gone. I told her of my visitor, the gray tiger with green eyes. My friend was a devoted cat person, so I had no doubts they would get on very well.

When I returned, my friend told me she had seen no sign of the cat. I flattered myself with the thought that the gray tiger was only interested in me and, knowing somehow that I was not there, didn't bother to come around. I was back three days and still there was no sign of her. I wondered if her people had moved and taken her with them.

Then one evening I heard a familiar cry. "I'm here!" But it lacked the old gusto. I looked out my window. It was still light. She was on the ground, looking up at me. "Oh, my God!" I began to tremble with rage and grief. She was skin and bones, dragging a back leg that looked broken. I could only imagine that she had been kicked or abused and starving since I'd been gone. She didn't have the strength to jump up to my windowsill, but cried, and looked at me with those green eyes. I ran out and tried to find the super to get the keys to let me into the back courtyard, but he was nowhere to be found. I tried to think what to do. It wouldn't do any good to enter the courtyard through another building because I couldn't get through the chain-link fence (or over it...it was topped with coils of barbed wire) that enclosed my alley. The gray tiger clearly hadn't the strength to scale the wall, as she had in the past, to come to me.

I came back in and looked out my window. It was now getting dark. I looked down at her and said, "If you can get up here, you know I will take care of you." She dragged herself back and forth in front of my window, wobbling, sometimes falling against the side of the building. She seemed to be gauging the awful distance up to my window, a distance she used to fly through without effort. "If you can make it up here, you know I'll take care of you," I said to her over and over. I watched as the little gray tiger, pitifully thin and broken, gathered her strength, her courage, and her *grit*. She shoved off with her one good back leg, stretched as best she could and managed to hook one paw over the bottom rung of my barred window. It was enough. I caught her and gathered her up into my arms. I had never seen such palpable will. She had accomplished something that she really wasn't physically capable of doing.

I made a soft bed for her in my bathroom, put food and water close to her, and jury-rigged a litter pan. After I had comforted her as best I knew how and saw that she ate something, I left her to sleep and called my vet. I explained the situation and was told to bring her in that night.

When the vet examined her, he discovered that her back leg was not broken, but that a large tumor was growing in the joint area. She was covered with lumps. He took a battery of tests and let her go home with me.

I never cursed my allergy as much as I did that night because I couldn't keep her with me. Fortunately, a friend offered her home for as long as we needed it. I took her in a cab to her new foster home. The vet had required that I give her a name when I registered her. I called her Seery. I had never called her anything before except little friend, kitty, and other such nonsense, for she was not my cat.

After two days, my friend reported that Seery was declining rapidly, refusing to eat and not responding to attention or affection. The vet, finally in possession of all the test results, called me, and explained that Seery was full of cancer. It was my decision of course but, since there was no treatment, I might want to consider putting her down.

I had seen her pain. She had come to me to do something. Was this the something she had in mind? I don't know. I made the decision to take her in the next day.

I picked her up at my friend's house. My friend walked me to the elevator, crying. I carried Seery in the cat carrier that I had brought her in. We took a long cab ride back to the veterinarian's office.

I held her in my arms while they inserted the IV. First, they administered a sedative. I could feel her relax and her green eyes held mine. I leaned close over her so she would see only me, my eyes looking into hers, and she wouldn't see the white-coated man behind me putting another needle into the end of the IV tube. It was painless and quick. Her mouth slacked open, her little pink tongue fell out, and the life left those green eyes. I felt quite sure she knew what was happening to her. I did not feel a sense of acceptance from her as much as resignation. I laid her down gently, still wondering if this is what she had come to me for. I burst into tears and ran out of the office.

She only had a name for three days, but I will always remember her as Seery, the gray tiger with the mystical, sea-green eyes who gave me so much of her friendship. She wasn't my cat. But I miss her.

Ellie and Me

"Ed! I'm going to meet her today," I chirped happily. "Her name is Ellie. I was told that she has a strong spirit that was never broken in spite of what she's been through, that she's difficult and eccentric."

Without missing a beat, Ed replied, "Honey, you couldn't have found a better match in a personals ad."

My friend Ed knew whereof he spoke.

I told him the rest of her story, as Sandy had told it to me. Sandy was a rescue society unto herself, specializing in small dogs. I had called her looking for a little dog, not a poodle, because I didn't want to compare him or her to Greta, my toy poodle who had been my companion for eighteen years and whom I was still mourning. Other than that, I wasn't particular about breed, pure or random. Sandy said, "How would you feel about a Shih Tzu?"

"I don't know. I've never known a Shih Tzu. They aren't really small, though, are they?"

"The one I have right now is. She is the smallest type of Shih Tzu—only nine pounds, and she has the prettiest little Shih Tzu face I've ever seen."

Then she described this little dog's past. The first two years of her life she had been confined to a kitchen, groomed to a fare-thee-well but never taken to a vet—a trophy dog, a decoration, never played with, never paid any attention, a joy to no one. That soon changed. The elderly couple that owned her were joined by their grown son who took his joy by abusing his parents' small dog. His sister, in an act of kindness, took the dog out of the house and left her at a shelter.

The shelter workers found themselves with a very pretty little dog who bit people. This lovely member of a breed known for its good nature had been turned into an aggressive, antisocial, biting dog—a piranha in a fur coat. Someone at the shelter called Sandy. "We aren't going to be able to place her...but there's something about her. We want to give her another chance." If Sandy wouldn't take her, they would have to euthanize her.

Sandy did take her, sent her to the vet for spaying and shots, and placed her with a nice family who, after a good try, brought her back. They couldn't deal with a dog with issues. Sandy was resigned to keeping her, even though she had pets of her own and was committed to fostering and placing other dogs. Ellie would be alive and not abused, but she wouldn't be "special."

I made an appointment to see the little dog with the pretty Shih Tzu face that afternoon.

This story is not about me, but suffice it to say, I know what it is to be neglected, humiliated, and powerless to do anything about it. I know what it feels like to have your back against a wall. I understand fear-biting.

During her first two days in my home, Ellie was aloof. She tolerated my picking her up and cuddling her and seemed more perplexed by it than anything else. "You can pick her up?" Sandy was incredulous when she called to see how things were going. She hadn't gotten near this little dog for the first few days Ellie had been with her, and for weeks, Ellie had stayed more or less out of sight, coming out at night to use the papers, eat, and drink.

Ellie mostly enjoyed our walks outside. In fact, the first time I opened the door to my apartment, she was out like a shot. I caught her in the lobby, thankful that no one had left the lobby door open to the busy street.

A week passed and I felt things were going smoothly. She never again made her mad dash out the door. She slept on the corner of my bed. She was eating well and did not seem afraid. Just aloof. I bought her toys and she learned to play tug and fetch. Playing was a new experience for her and she took to it with the first glimmers of joy I had seen in her.

I was always careful to give her plenty of warning when I was going to pick her up. Maybe this time I reached for her a little too fast and she snapped at me, without making contact. After the snap, she hit the floor in a crouch that indicated she expected me to hit her. I hunkered down next to her and spoke softly and clearly. "I will never hit you. No matter what you do. No matter what you do, you will always be my dog and I will never hit you." She relaxed. I stroked her head.

The inevitable day came when I had visitors, a friend and her husband. Ellie went wild, barking and attacking his feet when he came in. Michael was wearing heavy work boots, knew her history, and was cool about it. Her abuser had been a man and she was unforgiving. On the street, she barked at men, but she was always on a short leash and they just smiled or laughed at this little half-pint willing to take them on. I had tried to correct her but it was obvious after the incident with my friend's patient husband that we needed professional help.

I called Carol Benjamin, whose books on dog training I had read and liked. She was also writing some pretty good mystery novels. I thought it was a long shot, but she answered her own phone! She told me she no longer trained but she recommended her best student. He lived in New Jersey.

Stephen turned out to be a soft-spoken, gentle man whom I liked at our first meeting. He instructed me not to do anything to correct Ellie when he entered my apartment. He wanted to see her behavior for himself. She gave him the full treatment, barking, snarling, nipping at his feet. When he'd seen enough, I put collar and leash on her and she settled down by my side across the room from him. He and I talked for a while; then he said, "Okay, just hand me the end of her leash." I did so, and Ellie who had been sitting quietly, went crazy. Speaking sweetly and soothingly, Stephen very slowly and gently drew her in toward him, while at the end of the leash she fought like a tiger. I watched, a little teary eyed and full of admiration for her great courage in the face of terror; her defiance of a creature, who in the past had proven himself dangerous to her and who was twenty times her size. When she was close to him, he put his hand very lightly on her head and eventually she stopped struggling. He had never stopped talking to her and when she was still, he said, "I just wanted her to experience at least once that coming close to a man will not hurt. Let's let her heartbeat get back to normal now."

That was the last time the trainer held her leash. He made it a point to pet her a little during every lesson, which she allowed, but never enjoyed. He trained me to train my dog.

During our first session, I described the incident when she snapped at me and he told me how to handle it if it happened again, as he suspected it would. "Dogs are pack animals." I knew that. "They are only comfortable and secure when they know their place in the pack, and in this pack you have to be alpha female. You pay the rent. She can't. It has to be this way, and your dog will be happier knowing that." I didn't know that. "She will test you from time to time...that's what pack animals do...expect it, but never let her win. *Never* let her win," he repeated. Tough love. Never letting her win meant maintaining eye contact until she broke it. I could verbally express my outrage over her bad behavior and all I needed was that little sign of submission—Ellie's breaking eye contact first.

Our training went well, surprising even the trainer. She learned sit, stay, and heel in two lessons. As he predicted, she did snap at me again and I followed his instructions. I took her head in my hands, expressed my outrage (bad dog!) and stared at her until she looked away. Her will was strong! It took minutes of my acting the part of the alpha wolf for her to avert her eyes (all those acting lessons finally paid off), but our covenant was not broken. I did not hit her.

She is and will always be my dog, no matter what. We are a pack, a family, of which I am the alpha female. That means I will take care of her and protect her, and she will not bite the hand that feeds her. And to my great astonishment, after this incident I saw her visibly relax. She became, overnight, more secure and appeared, for the first time since I had met her, happy. Stephen was right.

That was the beginning of an extraordinary bonding between Ellie and me. Training, I discovered, is not only about getting a dog to do this or that; it is not even just about establishing a bond of trust and a pack hierarchy; it is, essentially, learning a common language. Once you know it, your dog and you, anything is possible.

She has learned to play and will now initiate play. She has grown to like being petted and scratched. She has learned that not all men "hurt." While she will always be wary of strangers, she seeks out Norberto, my doorman, and every evening they have their ritual, "Hi Ellie! How are you?" he croons in his thick Spanish accent. He scratches her head and her ears and her chest and she cranes toward him as if she can't get enough, actually as if no one else ever pets her. (*You don't have to enjoy it that much*, I often think, somewhat peevishly.) I have discovered what treats she likes and know her favorite chew toys. She has discovered that if she wants something, I will respond. I can tell when she wants to play, when she wants to go out, and when she wants to be left alone. After my surgery, she stayed tucked into my side on the bed during the long hours I was recuperating. After her surgery, I fed her by hand and gave her water out of a soup ladle. Sometimes, in the middle of the night, she wakes me with a nudge of her nose against my hand and cuddles in close. I don't know what precipitates this, because she is still not what you would call a "cuddly" dog. Maybe she's had a bad dream. I imagine she dreams that she is back in that kitchen, being alternately neglected and tormented, and she wants to reassure herself that she is here now, with me. Maybe she's just cold.

We have been together five years now. She is funny, playful, willful, spunky, but never outright disobedient. She hasn't "tested" me in a long time. There aren't many rules. The rules we have are for her own protection. Come. Heel. Sit and stay. No biting. She is less aggressive with strangers, but she will never be gregarious. That is fine with me. When I come home she is waiting for me at the door, all one joyful wiggle. Joy. What I brought to her life; what she brought to mine. A silver cord connects my heart to hers. I can feel it. If that sounds like something out of *Jane Eyre*, it is. *Jane Eyre* is the story of love between two damaged souls. There are all kinds of love. There is every kind of damage. The one universal is that the only cure for damage is joy.

Ellie lived six more years after this story was written, finally succumbing to cardiopulmonary disease. A hunk of my heart went with her.

The Bristol Dogs

PERHAPS IT WAS THE IMPLAUSIBLE drama; the extreme contrast from dark to light, warm to cold, death to life; the inexplicability of it and the impossibility of describing the depth and nature of my experience, but I never told anyone about it—this tiny event that unfolded as a gift from and a glimpse into a universe that is essentially loving. That's how it felt at the time. And still does.

To understand my enchantment, for that is what it was, one has to understand my feeling for dogs. Unless we hurt them and warp their natures, turning them insane—to either aggression or fearfulness—dogs are possessed of all the goodness and joy and altruism that humans only ever aspire to. I think dogs are the angels among us. I have experienced firsthand their intelligence, compassion, intuition; their living-in-the-moment joy; their loyalty and devotion.

The place is Bristol, South Dakota; the time, January during the three-day blizzard of 2012. I am staying in the nursing home where my mother is struggling to die. The nurses called me to come back from my home in New York. She is unresponsive, they told me. But she isn't. She bats their hands away if they so much as try to moisten her lips. She doesn't want to be touched. I don't know if she knows I'm here. I do know that she wouldn't care if she did. Her room is dark and foul with the rankness of her dying breaths. Her eyes are completely black from renal failure. I've never seen her so thin. I've never seen her without her teeth. The person in the bed looks nothing like my mother.

In my first novel, I wrote a scene in which Gustie, after sitting at the bedside of a dying loved one for days, ventures out and loses her way in a blizzard. She is guided home by deer who turn out to be phantoms—spirits of deer who no longer existed at that time in that place.

The blizzard ends and I go outside for my first walk since I began this deathbed vigil. The sky is sapphire blue over a landscape of brilliant, sparkling white, unbroken snow. I'm numb and feel disconnected from ordinary life.

I blink in the unmitigated brightness of snow and sun and sky, which seem to reflect each other, exponentially intensifying the brilliance of each. Shimmering white, ethereal white, a whiteness not possible in the big city where I live, a whiteness that bespeaks beginning-of-the-world purity and cleanliness stretches as far as I can see—a considerable distance as there is little to break the view. Bristol is a thriving little community, population 341. The nursing home perches on a small rise at the edge of town, and in a town this small, you are never far from wide-open spaces. Only the sidewalk around the nursing home has been shoveled, and only a small area in the parking lot has been cleared. Suddenly, as if materializing out of the light itself, in the distance appears a dark spot that, as it gets closer, takes the shape of a brown dog, laughing mouth, flapping tongue, bounding through the snow. He is barreling straight toward me, but I see he is a young Hershey lab and in any case, I'm not afraid of dogs. He is warm, as though cold and snow do not touch him. He leaps around me and up, resting his paws on my shoulders and I embrace him; swept into his luminous eyes, I return his smile. And then, out of the same ether appears a black dog, leaping joyously through the snow toward us. He is older, more filled out, but also warm and sleek. His eyes are dark, large, and lustrous, and I feel *seen*. My first thought is *Are you real?*

They clearly are friends and play with each other and with me, and even as I play with them and pet them and allow them to leap up on me, I am not sure that they are real dogs. I'm feeling a bit like the character in the novel of my own creation.

When their exuberance carries them off, bounding through the snow and out of my sight, I realize that my face is near frozen and I should go in. A lady in a wheelchair parked by the window greets me with, "I thought they were going to knock you down!" and then I know they were flesh and blood. When I ask one of the nurses who lives in Bristol about them, she tells me they are strays. Hunters often abandon their dogs here, she says. A woman feeds them and takes them in out of the cold.

They were not spirit dogs but dogs with spirit, the spirit of generous joy and friendship and delight in being alive. I'd never seen them before. I never saw them again. They came to me at just that moment as a gift. Nothing and no one living or dead could have refreshed me, comforted me, as they did.

Not the nursing home chaplain, a kind woman, my age or maybe older, who came into the room the day before, sat down (uninvited) and asked if she could pray with me. The asking was in such a way as to make me believe that *she* needed it, and I said "You can pray for my mother if you wish." It is not for me to deny others their prayers, their comfort, but, silently, I howled, *If God answered prayer, do you think my mother would be lying here like this, rasping out every breath, for days and days?* (Why does God have to be begged and cajoled into doing the right thing, anyway? And when He doesn't, why do we let Him off the hook?) So the chaplain prayed. I did not anymore. I fancied that she left, puzzled or pitying.

Had my mother's death been peaceful, serene, like the deaths described in all the books I'd read on dying or like I'd heard others describe the last moments of their loved ones ("she saw the Lord," "he saw the light"), I'd have maybe murmured a prayer, but it wasn't. Her dying was hard to the last second. She died with a snarl on her lips and black eyes that seemed to see the minions of hell coming for her. The nurse said, "This is often the case with Alzheimer's patients." I see. Then dying is wholly dependent on the dying person's state of mind. There is nothing objective at work here?

The nurses left me as soon as they had pronounced her dead. I tried to close her eyes. They would not close. *Even this!* I thought. She had never allowed me to do anything for her. Even this. I tried again and then left them for the undertaker or someone with pennies in her pocket.

What did the dogs do that the chaplain could not? They gave me the *experience* of joy, connection, beauty, fun, not just the wish for the promise of it. They showed me the other side of the nature of things. The sad side, the darker side I'd been living, in that dark, rank, room, and that is the nature of things—everything dies. Even stars. But the flip side is that what lives can live in joy. Asking the question, *Where's God in all this?* and trying to answer it, does not increase our happiness. Playing in the snow with a couple of dogs does.

Dolly

It was an August when dust rose out of the swamps. There were many such Augusts on the prairie. I remember a few of them. So hot, they made you long for the tear-freezing cold of January. So dry your lips cracked and your nose bled. And the dust. The surrounding marshlands dried to a powder and took to the air. Birds hunched, sullen, on crackling branches. Beings who crept and scurried lay low and still. The fish didn't bite. Only grasshoppers remained themselves in the torporific dryness; while all else withered and browned, out of sheer cussedness, they stayed fat and green, jumping crazily like odd shapes of viridescent corn popped off the hot skillet of the land.

The Dust. You could feel the grit between your teeth. It coated your eyeballs and gathered in black glutinous masses at the corners of your eyes. It didn't matter if you had a well that wasn't dry so there was water for the few head of stock, water for the washing and for the big tub in the kitchen on Saturday night. Dust like that—it gets into you. It makes your every breath a sigh and every sigh a prayer for rain. Dust like that can make you careless—make you lose your attention to the details of life so that you slog, stuporous, through days at a time, because the human soul needs greening and moisture.

On a farm, even that of a poor sodbuster like my great-grandfather, carelessness can be fatal. Through a failure of attention, he almost lost a child, and I was almost not born as the person I am—almost, but for a horse named Dolly.

Dolly wasn't much of a horse. Well, she couldn't have been much in the way of looks or breeding if Baathor and Mattie Halverson had her because they were dirt poor. My grandmother described Dolly to me as darkish brown with a bush of a tail and a thick mane that was a pleasure to get your fingers into. A big horse. Dolly pulled the wagon and the plow—when she felt like it. About half the time she didn't feel like it and then she would stop wherever she was for a quiet period of meditation. "You rotten horse," Baathor would utter with great feeling but between his teeth and under his breath, for he was by nature a quiet man. Soft curses would follow in Norwegian. He had no delicacy about swearing in English. He just never learned how. Then he would enact the ritual of pulling at her harness, pushing her, prodding her, and pleading with her before he stomped off, still cursing, to do something else for a while, or he would go into the house boiling mad, sit down to an early lunch of bread and milk and a little coffee, and between bites, mixing his English and his Norwegian, mutter over that rotten horse.

Not because she cared a thing for Dolly—she didn't—but because she was weary, overworked, never complained, and couldn't stand the complaints of others, Mattie would say, "Pa, you know nothing moves Dolly, so just eat now. She'll go again later on." And then she, standing over her sink, and he, bent over his bowl of bread and milk, would continue their murmuring, a soft little duet with neither of them listening to the other. "Might as well complain there's no sun in the middle of the night," she'd go on. "There just isn't, so that's all. There's no sun at midnight and nothing moves that horse. So there, then. Eat now." She would pour him a little more coffee and push the sugar bowl in his direction; he'd put a teaspoon of sugar in his mouth, drink down the rest of his coffee, and head back to Dolly who would now be ready to go.

When she worked, she *worked*. That horse pulled a plow, my grandmother said, like nobody's business. When she was hitched to the wagon, you never had to use the reins, and never the whip. When she got to this part of the story, Grandma's face turned serious, and her eyes misted a little. "No matter how mad he got, Pa never whipped her. I never saw him whip any animal. No sir." Even at eighty, she still adored her father, and I think she still missed him. "No, we never had to use the reins with Dolly. She knew where we were going and went there lickety-split—if she went at all." Here she would chuckle again, and add, her cornflower-blue eyes twinkling, "But one thing's for sure... she never made us late for church!" So Baathor never got rid of Dolly, mostly because he could not afford to replace her. A horse working half the time was better than no horse at all.

On this August evening the sun still burned hot and red, unrelenting in the endless sky. Baathor had only a few cows of his own. A couple of milkers and a dry one he was letting rest. But he had a good well. Either it was deep enough or in just the right spot, he didn't know which and he didn't care, he just thanked the Almighty for it, for he had plenty of water and the Molviks across the paper-dry swamp didn't; neither did the Petersons to the north. They gave him their cows to keep during the dry spell along with a little money for the trouble he was put to looking out for them.

Baathor's small weathered-wood barn opened on its south side into the corral. The corral gate opposite the barn opened out to the pasture. A big water trough stood next to the barn inside the corral. The cattle spent these hot nights in the corral. Only Dolly was put in the barn with her own water and the upper halves of the barn doors left open so she could get what breeze there was.

Every evening Baathor filled the trough, opened the corral gate, and whistled. The cattle, knowing water awaited them, needed no rounding up or herding. All he had to do was fill the trough, make sure the gate was open, whistle, and get out of the way. Every night it was near to a stampede to get to the trough.

There had been no plowing and no place to go, so Dolly had been turned out in the pasture for the whole day. This evening, in a dust-trance, Baathor entered the corral through the pasture gate instead of through the barn as he usually did. He left the gate open behind him. He went straight to the trough and began to pump the water. The water stubbornly refused to rise. He pumped hard, primed it, cursed it, pumped some more. Finally, the well begrudged him a trickle, then a small stream. He pumped steadily till the water gushed. The trough had been not even half full; he had a lot of pumping to do. He worked with a will, facing the barn, his back to the corral and to the rest of the yard, so he did not see his little girl who was just starting to walk venture out of the house. She toddled rapidly with baby glee at her mysterious freedom. Mama's hands did not swoop down and take her off course. Pa didn't seem to notice her either. She was free. She toddled in a straight line across the barnyard to the corral, crawled under the fence to the middle, and plopped down in her own little cloud of dust.

The water finally level with the rim of the trough, Baathor stopped pumping. Sweat ran into his eyes. In one motion, he wiped the sweat away with his forearm as he squinted up into the reddening sky, whistled, and turned to make sure the cattle had heard. He saw them coming, could already hear their hooves and feel the vibrations in the ground of the heavy bodies moving toward him before he saw his girl, happy in the cloud of dust that her small hands splashed up all around her, directly in the path of the thirsty herd. The corral wasn't wide, but it was long. He could not get to her before they did and he knew it.

I have always imagined my great-grandfather's feelings at that moment. Everything in that precise moment must have been in slow motion: the baby sitting in a pool of dancing dust made golden by shafts of evening sunlight, her skin, hair, and diaper covered with golden dust so that only her laughing mouth shone pink and her eyes a blue that rivaled the sky, while the cattle, a mass of huge brown and white and russet shapes, horns on some, all with hooves hard and sharp, crashed into each other and surged inexorably forward; heavy, ponderous—*how could they move so fast?* he wondered. Frozen in the deathly calm of the helpless and utterly despairing, Baathor saw it all.

Dolly saw it, too. With the speed that only a horse can muster—even the most ordinary of horses can call upon the blood and bones of the Thoroughbred when she needs to run, when she *must* run—Dolly ran. She galloped across the pasture, cut in front of the cattle, and slipped through the gate just ahead of them to where the child giggled and played in the dust. Planting her four legs like cedars around the baby, she stood her ground.

Grandma knew Dolly. She had sat on her back and played with her mane. When Baathor did chores in the barn, she played in Dolly's manger stroking her velvet nose and babbling baby language, while Dolly nodded her big head in perfect understanding. She had no fear of the giant horse and stayed safe within the forest of Dolly's legs. The cows thundered around the horse bumping her flanks as they went by, but nothing moved Dolly.

The clock began ticking again for Baathor. Jumping the fence in time to keep from being mashed against the barn, he ran sobbing around the corral and scrambled back over the fence. He scooped up his baby and sobbed into her neck, then he sobbed into Dolly's neck. The cows, ignoring horse, man, and child, nuzzled and jostled each other for position around the trough, some of them were already muzzle-deep in the water.

All the while my little grandma had been having the time of her life, and still was; now she was high enough to get her fingers entwined in Dolly's mane. Mattie, in her own trance, with three other children to mind and supper to get on the table, had only now noticed that her youngest was missing and came outside to find her husband crying into Dolly's mane. Wide-eyed she reached over the fence. He disentangled the child's hands from the horsehair and handed her to her mother. He took out his handkerchief, wiped his muddy, tear-streaked face, and blew his nose. He could hardly tell her what he'd done. He could hardly speak for what had almost happened. The cows, sated now, were placid and looked about without interest as Baathor led Dolly to the water. "Come on ole girl. Get your water." His voice still quivered.

Grandma said that nobody complained after that when Dolly took her rests. "Nothing moves Dolly" was now spoken with pride and awe to the neighbors. Even after she could no longer pull a plow or wagon, while other horses were being bought and sold, Dolly roamed the pasture or munched sweet oats while a young girl sat on her back, braiding and unbraiding her mane, sometimes weaving colored yarns among the coarse hairs, and sharing secrets that only Dolly could understand.

To the Little Brown Snake I Encountered in the Driveway of United Jersey Bank in the Meadowlands

I EXPECTED YOU TO SLITHER away. I intended that you should (I wanted you off the road where you would not be fodder for the unforgiving treads of a tire). So small and new to life, you rose to face me in a delicate spiral; your tiny black tongue darted defiance—at *me*, a giant in your world.

I don't know what kind of snake you are in your sleek suit of herringbone tweed. I don't know much about snakes except that the serpent nation carries the burden of human fear and hatred.

It was not always so. Once you were chosen the symbol of healing, but even that we turned into the very logo of evil, as healing art transmogrified and spawned the pain giver—the vivisector.

Little brown snake, such courage in a tiny new being—I marvel. Lovely, aerodynamically perfect, secure in yourself, you rest in your spiral and will not be moved—will not skitter off in fright at my gentle nudging, at my monstrous presence, at my foolish attempts to shoo you back into the tall grass.

Should I pick you up and put you there? It is cold and damp in the sheltering weeds, and you will only seek the warmth of the pavement once again. It is after five. I see no cars. Perhaps there will be no more killing wheels today. So I will spare you that indignity and leave you your autonomy.

I wish you long life. May the Tailor fashion you many such tweedy suits as you grow. May you take your leisure through golden days on warm rocks safe from tires and frightened humans with gunnysacks, sticks, and knives.

Little brown snake, may you live your life free from the terrible burden that Man-Symbol-Maker has placed on your kind—for we have laid upon your slender form all that we fear and loathe in ourselves. Little brown snake....

For nearly four years in the early 1990s, the author was a volunteer for POWARS[3] in New York City. In the following two accounts, the names (and some other details) have been changed to comply with a confidentiality agreement, but the stories are true.

---

3   *POWARS is the acronym for Pet Owners with HIV/AIDS Resource Service, Inc., an organization staffed at every level by volunteers, founded in 1988, and supported by donations. If a client could afford a fee, they paid it. Most of our clients had been wiped out financially, however, and no one was ever turned down because they couldn't pay.*

We provided pet care services for people who were HIV positive. What this meant at that time was, really, people with full blown AIDS who could no longer care for their companion animals themselves. The POWARS decade spanned the apex of the AIDS epidemic when, often, a person with AIDS had few or no friends left and all too often had been abandoned by family. His or her (yes, we had women clients) only source of affection and warmth came from their companion animals. The mission of POWARS was to keep a client and their pet together until the client passed away (and back then, no one survived), and then we placed the animal in a new loving forever home if that was necessary. It was often necessary, because either no friends or family were left or they couldn't care for a pet.

We walked dogs (sometimes as often as three or four times a day); we changed litter pans, hydrated cats, took dogs and cats to grooming and veterinary appointments (and often paid the bill); we delivered food and cat litter (and often paid the bill). POWARS had fund raising events and many times, volunteers reached into their own pockets to buy something they knew a client needed—even if it was not strictly pet-related (I knew of volunteers who brought groceries when they noticed bare cupboards). Many suppliers, groomers, and veterinarians offered us special rates. We also provided foster care for pets when clients were in the hospital.

By the time I joined as dog walking coordinator, we served all five boroughs.

I now live in a small town and I have heard, since I came back, the sentiment frequently expressed that people in small towns take care of each other. While that's true, it still raises my hackles. People in big towns do too. In New York City, I saw hundreds and hundreds of people helping people who were total strangers. Our volunteers got little thanks and gave hours of their time and much of their treasure. In a small town, people know who you are (and you are probably related to a third of them), and if you have an opportunity to help and you don't— people will know. They will know if you do help and think well of you. In New York City, nobody knows or cares what you do. I fell in love with New Yorkers the first time (the second time was 9/11) during my tenure with POWARS, because I saw that our volunteers—who came from all walks of life, all genders, all sexual orientations, all economic and social classes, all educational backgrounds—were the most genuine, generous, caring people I had ever known. They stepped up at a time when there were no official agencies or social workers assigned to people living with AIDS. Even after the formation of Gay Men's Health Crisis, the pets were afterthoughts. POWARS changed all that for NYC (San Francisco already had such an organization). Our volunteers came forward for hands-on work with animals belonging to people who were society's pariahs during a time when some still thought you could contract HIV from a toilet seat. POWARS volunteers ventured into strange (and often risky) neighborhoods, into strange people's homes, bringing care and comfort to the only ones left who brought care and comfort to people with AIDS—their dogs and their cats (we even had a bird and a turtle on our list for a time). I look back on it: it was painful work; it was good work; and it is still the best thing I have ever done.

POWARS was dissolved in late 1998.

Luke

BOTH KURTIS AND DANNY ARE at the hospital. Kurtis is a patient and Danny, who recently returned from a stint as a patient himself, keeps vigil by his partner's side. I let myself into their apartment with keys left at the desk.

Luke is stretched across the foot of the bed. His head is raised. He looks composed and regal. Anticipation flickers, then fades in his eyes as he realizes it is only me, a volunteer—not one of his Beloveds. But, with the innate good manners of the golden retriever (Luke is more red than gold—perhaps his lineage boasts a bit o' the Irish), he tosses his head and smiles (yes, dogs *do* smile), bounds off the bed, and is before me in one leap. I tap my chest. He rises up, places a paw on each of my shoulders, and nuzzles my cheek while I put my arms around him and drivel, "Hey boy, good boy, are you my sweet Lukey Lukey Lukey?" and other such nonsense into his ear, because I've lost my heart to this guy.

Back on all fours, he spins some tight, gleeful circles, slowing long enough for me to slip the collar over his head. Danny's note says the door locks by itself. I close it behind us and off we go.

Central Park is in its autumnal glory. Luke, in his shining, reddish-gold coat, could have been picked by

Central Casting to make his appearance here this day. Leaves rustle at our feet. The trees are still ablaze with yellows, golds, and reds, and leaves leaves leaves flutter softly earthward all around us. The season of abundance: of colors; of contrasts—toasty fires and brisk air; cold cheeks and warm, gloved hands; traditional gatherings of family and friends and the thorn of loneliness. There is heightened awareness of *moments*, and Luke fills this moment for me. His jaunty grace and benevolent expression turn heads and call forth smiles from everyone who looks at him.

We trot along, making good time on the outside track of the reservoir, which is also a bridle path. We are careful not to frighten the horses. (Dogs are not allowed on the inside track, closest to the fence overlooking the water. We decide this is just snooty prejudice but abide by the rule nevertheless.)

Other dogs approach. Luke is reserved and friendly, but he's no pussycat when challenged. I keep a firm grip on his leash.

My right shoe begins to flop. Loose laces. "Whoa, Lukey." I pull off my gloves. "Here, Luke. Hold these." He takes the gloves in his mouth and I retie my shoes. When I put out my hand, he gives the gloves back.

Luke gives me a run for my money on the straightaway, but as we head down a steep incline he slows immediately and looks over his shoulder to check how I'm doing. Can't be too careful with a middle-aged lady in sneakers with loose laces.

We've been all around the reservoir. We are losing light and it's time to leave the park.

When we get back, Danny is sprawled across the bed. His face brightens as he sees his dog. "Hi, Honey," he says, caressing the golden's head. Luke gives him a warm and gentle greeting, then dives ungently into his dinner bowl, which Danny has prepared for his return.

I briefly describe a few highlights of our walk and, because Danny always asks, assure him what a good dog Luke is.

Then Danny tells me, "You do a wonderful service. Without you guys at POWARS, we'd have to give him up." Such open gratitude embarrasses me (POWARS orientation sessions stress that we are not to expect and are unlikely to get gratitude and if that's what we are looking for, we should not be there).

I stammer, "Well, uh...that's what we're here for." Then he says, "You know, Luke knows when Kurtis isn't coming home at night, because then he sleeps next to me on the bed. He never does that any other time. He seems to know what's going on. It's like...he knows what I need."

Of course, he does.

I leave then, but before I get to the end of the long hall to turn the corner for the elevators, I hear Danny's voice, "Honey. Honey." I turn, thinking Luke has followed me out the door, though I was sure I closed it behind me. But there is Danny with a small bouquet of flowers in his hand. "Honey, I forgot. I wanted to give you these."

I walk back to him. "I thought Luke was Honey," I say.

Danny says, "He's Little Honey. You're Big Honey."

I thank him for the flowers.

In the next several months, the condition of both men deteriorates rapidly. Danny has now been in the hospital for two weeks and Kurtis is the one at home.

Kurtis, more reserved than Danny, is usually lying fully clothed, but clearly all in, on the bed when I come for my scheduled walk. The door is open, so when I knock, he says, "come in" and doesn't have to get up to let me in.

Luke is always waiting for me in the middle of the floor, wagging his tail expectantly as I grab the leash off the hook and call him to me. He whirls a couple of times in his happy circles and then sits while I fasten his collar.

Danny's hospital stay lengthens and Kurtis's routine with all the volunteers is the same. The door is open. He is resting on the bed and nods as we enter and prepare Luke for his walk. When we return the dog, Luke's bowl is full of food and Kurtis is back on the bed. We let ourselves out.

Today, my scheduled walk is the last one of the day instead of the first.

I arrive about 9:00 in the evening. The door is ajar, so I say "hello" and enter the apartment. Luke is waiting for me in the middle of the room, as usual, wagging his tail. Kurtis is not on the bed, so I assume he is feeling stronger today and is perhaps in the laundry room or picking up his mail.

When we return about an hour later, the door is still ajar, as I left it, and there is still no Kurtis in the room. I unfasten Luke's collar and hang it on the hook. But there's something...something is not quite right. I pause. I step farther into the room. The apartment, which is always pristine, tidy, and fresh, smells a little stale. It is not a smell that I have ever encountered in this spanking-clean place. I take a few more steps into the apartment, so I can see around the corner into the bathroom.

Kurtis is draped over the rim of the tub, his head hidden by the shower curtain. He is nude. He is dead. In death, his bowels have loosened and emptied onto the tile floor.

Luke is showing no particular distress. I don't know how long Kurtis has been dead. I touch his back. It is as cold as the porcelain tub. I am hyperventilating and manage to dial 911, and then I call Elizabeth, Danny and Kurtis's case manager. She arrives only minutes after the uniformed police officers, followed by the EMTs and a plainclothes detective who looks uncannily like Dennis Farina, the actor who plays a New York detective on a popular television show. Elizabeth shows them Kurtis's case file and tells them what I already have, that he was in the final stages of AIDS. The detective sees no reason to stay; they are already ruling this a natural death, though Elizabeth and I suspect a suicide.

The uniformed officer who was first on the scene opened desk drawers and found Kurtis's address book. He calls a number. "Is this Mr. Treadman? Are you Kurtis's father?" The officer lowers his voice and hangs up so quickly, I don't know what they could have arranged in that time. Elizabeth speaks to the officer and nods her head sadly. She comes back to sit next to me.

"What did he say?" I whisper. The officer informed Kurtis's father that his son was dead and asked what arrangements they should make for the body. Kurtis's father said, "I don't care what you do with it. Throw it in the river."

Luke goes home with a friend of Danny and Kurtis's for the next few days until Danny returns from the hospital and volunteer walks are resumed.

It is clear to all of us now that Luke is really Danny's dog. As Danny declines physically, he spends more and more time in bed. He has twenty-four-hour home-health care; his friend, Sean, stays every other night and supervises the home care; Danny's brother and sister-in-law spend every other week with him, traveling up to New York from their home and jobs and children in Alabama; and he has Luke, who never leaves his side except when he is walked or fed.

We volunteers know how Danny is on any given day without having to see him. All we have to do is observe Luke. On days that Danny feels better, Luke is buoyant. On Danny's bad days, Luke's head hangs low and his feet are heavy.

When it is my turn to walk Luke, the home-care attendant always has his leash snapped on and she just hands him through the door to me, so I don't have a chance to see or talk to Danny himself. But one day, Danny is seated in the chair opposite the door. I go in and sit next to him at the end of the sofa. His appearance shocks me. He is suffering from what they call wasting. There is no flesh, only skin, on the bones of this once robust, handsome, young man, who could have modeled for Marlboro Man commercials. I take his hand. It is just a pile of little bones. "Hello, Danny."

"Hello," he smiles his sweet Danny smile. Luke sits before us, close, gently wagging his tail. "He's a bear isn't he?"

"Yes, he is," I say. "A cuddly bear."

"He's very nice," Danny says. "Do you know who he belongs to?"

"He's yours, Danny. He belongs to you. You belong to him."

Danny smiles happily. I am deeply shaken. I did not know that he was in dementia. I believe it's what Kurtis feared for himself and is why he killed himself before its full onset.

I take Luke out in the mornings. His morning routine never varies. He waits till we get to Riverside Park and goes to a special spot and relieves himself. Then we walk about twenty minutes south. The twenty minutes back, plus the time it takes to get to and from the park gives him over an hour out of the apartment in the fresh air with a bit of exercise. We do this rain or shine.

But this morning, Lukey does his thing on his spot and we walk not even five minutes when he stops. He has never done this before. "Don't you want to walk today, Luke?"

He turns around and leads me back to the apartment. The home-care worker is surprised to see us. I hand her his leash and shrug. "I don't know. He didn't want to walk today."

I go to work and shortly after I arrive at my office, Sean calls, crying. Danny has just died. Luke got back in time to be close beside him when he died. Had we taken our long walk, he would not have been back in time. He knew. Somehow, he knew.

Danny's brother and his wife adopted Luke and took him back with them to their home in Alabama. I got a Christmas card from them every year with a picture of a happy Luke, surrounded by grass and trees and kids. Years later, they left a message on my machine, the day Luke died.

Chumbly

I HAD BEEN WARNED. INDEED, that's why I was there in the first place. A client's friend called to say she was taking care of Martin's lorikeet Chumbly, but the bird bit her. Chumbly would not let her change the water or clean his cage. He was vicious. She was afraid of him and she had had enough. "POWARS has to do something!" she demanded.

How bad can this be? I wondered. What are we talking about here? A giant condor? I was willing to give it a try, even though this bird was out of my neighborhood and did not fall within my volunteer job description as the dog walking coordinator. The relevant case manager could not be reached, and Steve, the Executive Director of POWARS, started calling everyone on his list. On this bright Saturday morning, I was the only one who picked up the phone. Of course, I had to go.

Before I did, however, I managed to get hold of a bird expert at the Bronx Zoo. I described the situation. She said, "Don't wear gloves. You'll only freak the bird out even more."

"Oh. Okay. No gloves. Bare hands it is."

As soon as I stepped over the threshold the screeching began. It sounded like something had escaped from hell and didn't like the new place any better. "Oh, Lord." I took a deep breath and proceeded cautiously into a small, simply furnished apartment. There, dominating the tiny living room, was a massive cage on a steel pedestal. Within the cage was a beautiful bird: Christmas red-and-green plumage, a curved ebony beak, hooky claws, and he was not happy.

Chumbly was flat against the bars, wings spread, eyes flaming (well, maybe they didn't actually flame—you had to be there), filling the place with his ear-splitting screeches. That curved black beak gave me pause.

I stared for a minute, wondering what in the world I was going to do first. The papers on the cage bottom were unspeakably filthy, as were his water and food bowls. No way was I not going to change them. But how?

I am in the habit of talking to plants and animals. It has never occurred to me that they don't listen. I began to talk to Chumbly, who continued to screech and flap and flame. "Okay, little birdfriend, here we go," I said as I tried to lift the top part of the cage. I hoped to place it with Chumbly in it on the papers I had spread out on the floor. Then I could thoroughly clean the tray that was the cage bottom. But the cage was too heavy. I simply could not lift it, even standing on a chair to get some leverage.

I called and left an urgent message at the POWARS office asking for phone numbers of volunteers in the neighborhood. It was obvious that I needed help. Then it occurred to me that if I tipped the cage just a little, I could slide the dirty papers out and push clean papers in. This would not result in the neatest appearance but it would give Chumbly a clean floor. So, bit by bit, section by section of the New York Times (this was during the Republican convention—the Republicans found themselves on the bottom of Chumbly's cage, face up), I moved slowly around the cage, pulling out the old, sliding in the new. When I had gotten all the way around, it didn't look too bad—kind of a ruffled effect that I found quite charming. Chumbly must have thought so, too, because by this time he had stopped screeching and was merely watching me with flaming eyes, hooked beak at the ready. He seemed relieved to be able to sit on the bottom of his home without getting soiled and soggy. All the while I was talking to him: "It's okay little Chumbly Chumbly theretherelittle birdiebirdie Chumbly boy sweetieboypie." I think that animals either feel sorry for me because I talk like an idiot, or they like my tone of voice, which is just a little musical and soothing. Whatever.

Next, I prepared Chumbly's food. This involved mixing up a special cereal paste and washing some fresh lettuce and grapes. I gave him the grapes first. I offered them one by one through the bars. With great delicacy, he took each grape in his beak and climbed to the top of his cage, where a large running shoe was affixed. He sat in the shoe to eat each grape, then climbed back down for the next one. Very cute. Chumbly was by now calm and dedicated to eating. I put the rest of the grapes on the bottom of his nice clean cage and reached in quickly for his food bowl. Chumbly was happily sitting in his shoe, munching a grape, and left my flesh unscathed.

I scrubbed his bowl, filled it with the cereal and lettuce and just as quickly replaced it on the bottom of the cage.

Chumbly's water bowl was not going to be as easy as the food bowl, for it was screwed onto the perch. My naked hand had therefore to remain inside the cage long enough to unscrew the thing. I continued to croon nonsense to Chumbly, who was no doubt relieved to have something other than the Republicans to listen to (the television had been left on for him for company).

As I was unscrewing the water bowl, Chumbly climbed out of his shoe and down to the perch and sidled over. I was in the process of unfastening the water bowl and I didn't want to make any sudden moves, so I just kept my hand still, hoping that I could withdraw without bleeding too much on my clean papered cage floor. In a strange and touching move, he licked the back of my hand. (Bird tongues, I discovered, are tubular.) Then he nestled the side of his head against my hand, much as a kitten would do. I cupped his head in my palm and he continued to nestle. "Oh, sweetiebirdpie, are you lonely?" Thereafter, getting the container out, and returning it clean and filled with fresh cool water, was a piece of cake.

I spent the rest of my time there, about an hour and a half, petting Chumbly's head, smoothing his wing feathers, and chucking him under the chin. When the POWARS office called me back, I could happily report I no longer needed help and that I was in the presence of the sweetest little bird in the universe.

When I spoke to volunteers who had an interest in dog walking, I told them that dogs understand on some level a great deal of what is happening around them, and they react, each in her own way, to these events. I would now say the same thing about birds. Not that I wouldn't have said it before, because my previous experience with birds, though limited and never with a lorikeet, convinced me that they are very smart cookies.

Chumbly was frightened, lonely, and upset. His human was ill and taken from him suddenly. More by accident than design, since I was not a bird expert, he received some comfort from my visit and was demonstrably appreciative. His unremitting show of affection, and perhaps, gratitude, touched me.

I was able to visit with him only once more before his companion returned home. But I won't forget this bright soul who gave me so much in return for some fresh newspaper and a few grapes.

ESSAYS

People Who Love Dogs

THE FRATERNITY/SORORITY OF DOG PEOPLE is a special one. I don't mean the people who buy dogs from breeders and that's the end of their involvement—with their own pampered pet; though, if the animal is well cared for, for his or her lifetime, that's good. These people in my opinion do not love dogs. They love their own dog. They love what dogs do for them; they love how dogs make them feel. Well, we all love that. But, I'm talking about the people who slog on in an almost endless sea of suffering animals, getting their hands dirty and their hearts broken, saving all they can, letting go the ones they can't. Whether you are involved in animal rescue in a network or a shelter or are one who brings rescues into your home, one at a time, adopting or fostering, you belong in this community of loving-kindness.

I know people who only adopt old dogs. The dogs no one else will adopt. Does it get easier to make the decision to let them go? No. Tears fall every single time. Every single time, parting is wrenching. But they do it again, and again. Taking care of old dogs or blind dogs or any dog with special needs does not require a soft heart—but a strong one. An open one.

The Iditarod

BILLED AS "THE LAST GREAT race," the annual dogsled race from Anchorage to Nome inspires passionate debate among those who have witnessed the event, either in all its happy glory or all its grim cruelty, depending on their point of view.

One assertion for the race not being as bad as critics declaim is that tourists and cameras are everywhere, all the time, and kennels are open to the public. Whether or not the public views or the cameras record all there is to see is a fruitless discussion for those of us who cannot go on-site. However, without recounting conflicting opinions and accounts (available in voluminous quantity on the Internet) some points are evident.

The Iditarod bears no resemblance to the run it purports to commemorate. The original trail of 674 miles was covered by twenty teams, running in relays. In today's Iditarod, a single team must cover the entire distance of 1,200 miles.

Iditarod supporters maintain that nothing short of the bond between Timmy and Lassie exists between all mushers and their dogs. Such bonds may frequently exist, but cannot be assumed. Because one works with dogs, or relies upon them for livelihood, it does not preclude disposing of (in harsh environments, this usually means killing) them when they are inconvenient. (Proof of this is the shooting to near extinction of the Inuit dog by the Arctic hunters when they were introduced to the snowmobile in the 1970s.) Even the hero dog Balto was sold to a vaudeville show by the very musher he made famous. Accounts of mushers beating and kicking to death dogs who lose them races, while not provable in every instance, ring plausible (some have been documented). Given what we know of human nature and animal cruelty as it is found in the lower forty-eight, there is no reason to suppose that Alaskan mushers are uniquely endowed with Franciscan regard for their animals.

Maintaining a kennel is costly, so even a large purse won't make a musher rich. If the money is all you race for, you probably can't afford the hobby. Pride and prestige can be powerful forces, certainly, but again, cannot be thrown up as proof that all mushers are ruthless in their drive to win. However, dogsled racing (the Iditarod in particular) has been described by participants as a powerful addiction. In addiction of any kind, reason plays no part. Winning the race becomes a fix as much as running it. This is perhaps the aspect of the Iditarod that might make a musher ruthless.

While arguments rage back and forth about what constitutes cruelty and what degrees of cruelty are manifest in the Iditarod, *both sides agree on one thing: dogs die in this race.* While it is likely that the number of dead and injured dogs is neither as low as claimed by race fans nor as high as implied by detractors, NO DOG SHOULD DIE FOR SPORT, just as no animal should be injured or die to make a film. Until the death and injury rate is zero (now, *at least* one dog dies *every year* in this race), this controversial race needs more careful investigation, more scrupulous monitoring, and more responsible reporting.

Priceless Legacy

Living with Lily, My Blind Dog

(This article first appeared in Grey Muzzle Organization's newsletter April 2011)

LIVING WITH A BLIND DOG is neither as difficult as you may fear nor as easy as you might hope. I have lived with Lil, my blind Shih Tzu, for several years and offer some recommendations that will work for all dogs. The modifications, variations, and add-ons (for dog age, size, temperament, environment, and so on) are just that—add-ons to these basics:

Mindfulness
Compassion
Cheerfulness
Your hands
Your voice
A short leash

The variations and add-ons will depend on many factors:

Your dog's size, age, and state of general health
High energy or low, or in between?

Is your dog dominant or submissive by nature?

Confident or fearful?

Do you live in a big house with stairs and a yard, or a small apartment in a busy city?

Do you have other dogs and/or cats?

Was your dog blind from birth, or did she become blind suddenly or gradually?

Has she always been your dog, or is she a recent member of your family?

Addressing each point is beyond the scope of this article, but you have resources, even a support group (find links at the end of this article). You're not alone, so don't panic.

Lily came to me about 95 percent blind. When she went completely blind within two years of my adopting her, she entered a period of depression—

> Your blind dog needs a quiet, private space of her own, a bed in a quiet corner or a closet she can always access, where she will not be disturbed.

and adjustment—where she felt safest in her closet, her own private cave where, I believe, feeling the limited space around her gives her a sense of security. I did not force her out of it. She came out willingly to eat and I coaxed her out for walks. This period lasted about six months. Now she still goes in there for naps or for the night, but just as often, she doesn't.

This is my first time in a relationship with a dog who is not constantly focused on me. Lily has to use all of her remaining senses, all of her own mindfulness, just to navigate in the world. I am here to make the way as easy and as comfortable for her as I can. That does not mean feeling sorry for her. To give her the best life possible, I balance between being aware of and accommodating her disability with

> Put yourself in your dog's place. While this does not mean applying human psychology to your canin's behavior, common sense will tell us what things are scary when we are only a foot tall and totally blind.

compassion and patience and not turning her into some kind of pampered, neurotic little invalid.

For example, when I first got her, with her limited vision she did not want to walk outside. Who could blame her? I live on a busy Manhattan street. She was paper trained. I could have left her in her comfort zone, languishing forever in my small apartment just looking forward to her next meal. I determined this would not be her whole life.

In time, we learned together to have a pleasant walk. Then she went completely blind, and we had to start all over again! But she now walks with me on the streets, sniffing everything. The first

> Be Alpha! Let your dog know you are in charge. Let her relax into your leadership. When there is a vaccum in the pack, a dog will try to fill it. In modern society, no dog can and certainly no blind dog. Trying will make them neurotic. Being alpha goes along with keeping them safe. When they trust that you will keep them safe on the streets, they will be more eager to go for walks with you. If you make a mistake now and then, don't beat yourself up. Dogs are more forgiving of their leaders than we humans are of ours. But don't make too many, or you will lose their trust.

time we went to the park, she was totally disoriented in a place without sidewalks or curbs. That required another, shorter, period of adjustment. Now she enjoys sniffing in the grass and dirt.

I keep the leash short. She is in roughly the heel position all the time, where she has the security of knowing that if she trusts that space and that tension on the leash, I won't let her run into anything. I tried a halter on her, but she was stressed and disoriented in it. Though the books recommend halters (for many dogs, this may be the right choice), Lily relies on the feeling of the collar on her neck. The slightest pressure she responds to and I can guide her easily through an intricate obstacle course. This is crucial on a New York City sidewalk where there are deep cracks in the cement, grates, garbage cans, newspaper dispensers—you name it—or in the park around twigs or stones. Occasionally, I have been momentarily distracted and she has bumped into something (we travel at a slow pace so she is never hurt). I feel terrible. She doesn't dwell on it. She spends no time with "Oh I bumped into that, I'm always bumping into

> A blind dog has no blink reflex. Be careful when you are in an environment where there is foliage of any kind. What may look like a harmless twig, vine, or pile of leaves could damage her cornea.

> In my small apartment, I do not wear shoes, ever. With a medium-size or big dog, stepping on them is not an issue. With a very small dog, it's always an issue as she is often right by my feet when I don't know she's there. In bare or stocking feet, I will feel her before I step down hard enough to hurt her.

something, my life is awful," creating a story around it the way I do when I have a mishap.

I've often read that dogs "make up for being blind" with other senses. Nonsense! A blind dog can't make up for anything anymore than a blind person can. They rely on their other senses more, but that's different from the idea that somehow the other senses expand to fill in the gap left by blindness. *You* have to fill that gap. You are her seeing-eye person. My dog is more careful, more mindful. Our walks are enjoyable, but they also take more mental energy from both of us. She is exhausted after every walk, even though I am guiding her every step. **No miracle happens that you and she do not create together, every step you take.**

My friend Doris has had two blind dogs and says, "Nothing was ever moved in my house while they were alive." This is not an issue in my tiny apartment, but if you must rearrange furniture, it's best to guide your dog around the place a few times on a leash so she can re-map the space in her head.

Small sounds in the apartment startle Lily. She does not do well in wind and sort of shuts down, perhaps because she can't hear as well in the wind and it is just a sensory overload. She has adjusted to soft rain, though not without a lot of gentle coaxing over the years—and a nice raincoat. I don't force her to go farther than necessary in inclement weather.

If she trusts that I am confident, she relaxes. If she knows from my energy that I am in control, then she doesn't have to be. In crowds, I pick her up and carry her. I did that with my sighted Shih Tzu as well. Not everyone is mindful of where they step. I don't like small dogs in crowds. It makes me nervous for them, so rather than communicate that nervousness to my dog, or put her at risk, I just pick her up and we walk through safely and securely. With a larger dog, this would not be an issue. Know your own dog.

Sometimes, even in a familiar space, or when doing a familiar thing, your dog may become suddenly disoriented. If there is no risk to her (and she should never be in a dangerous situation—that's your responsibility) and she can work her way out of it, let her. But use your good judgment and knowledge of her. A little stress occasionally can be stimulating, but too much too often is bad. Lily sometimes gets into a corner or walks under a wood chair and can't find her way out. I can read when she is going to panic or just give up or when she's going to slowly reorient herself and go out the way she went in. If she is headed for a panic or a shut down, I gently guide her out of the corner or the chair slats with a cheerful, "There you go." And that's it. No after story from either of us. No "Oh why did I do that!"

"Check your bowl" means I have put her food there. Often it takes her a while to find it even though her water and food bowls are always in the same place. If it takes her too long, and she has somehow become disoriented, I will point her in the right direction. You have to judge when letting them work something out is best for them and when it's just unnecessary stress that you can easily fix. Mindfulness.

Talk to your dog more than you would to a sighted dog. This tells them where you are and is especially important on a walk. Even though the slight tension on the leash orients Lily to where I am, she is visibly happier and more confident when I talk to her more. We also have guide words.

> Encountering other dogs, even the dogs in your own family group, can be problematic, because your dog can't give the right physical signals nor see the signals other dogs are sending. Be mindful, be careful and ready to take immediate action if there is any sign of danger to your dog.

Pausing and then the word "step" means we're at a curb or step. "Step up," the same. "Wait" means just that, so she doesn't bump into the lobby door while I'm getting my keys out to open it. In front of our apartment, I don't have to say anything because the floor texture changes. When she steps from the tiles to the carpet, she pauses without the word. We did not have any training sessions per se. I just use the same words every time for everything we do. To avoid startling her, I say "pick you up" before I pick her up, "pet you" before I touch her. "Go for walky?" before I put on her leash and just my hand on her back before I put on her coat or sweater. On the street, if she pauses and doesn't want to move forward for some reason, and I see that she's all right (even a blind Shih Tzu can be willful at times!), I just say "walkies" in a bright, high-pitched tone. I use this word instead of "heel" because on a noisy street she can hear it better and it's more cheerful sounding (though it may make me look ridiculous; it worked for Ms. Woodhouse[4] and it works for me too!). The word doesn't matter, but it should come naturally to you so you use it every single time.

Consult all the resources available, but your responsibility first, last, and always is to KNOW YOUR OWN

DOG. Use common sense. Some suggestions I read seem absurd or even wrong. For example, one book recommends using poles to guide a blind dog (and certain paraphernalia supposed to serve as white canes for canines). The other book advises never to do this! I agree with the second book, as touching Lily with anything but my hands would confuse and frighten her. You have to be mindful of your dog and pay careful attention to her. You will not get it right 100 percent of the time, but over time the two of you will fashion a routine and physical environment within which she can live happily and with the lowest possible stress.

Perhaps your blind dog came to you frightened, timid, shaking with fear or nervous aggression; or perhaps, if she went blind in your care, began her unsighted life depressed, unwilling to leave her bed in the closet—the joy of seeing her wag her tail on a walk, sniff every pole, street sign, or blade of grass, and happily navigate your home on her own, will fill you up. The fruits of being truly mindful with your dog at all times will be, perhaps, that you learn to live a more mindful, compassionate life. And that will be her lasting and priceless legacy to you.

Resources:

Support group for people with blind dogs: http://pets. groups.yahoo.com/group/blinddogs/

Blind Dog Rescue: http://www.blinddogrescue.org/

Tips from Blind Dog Rescue: http://www.blinddogrescue. org/aboutblinddogs/blinddogtips.html

Old Dog Haven has an info sheet on blind dogs. "SUGGESTIONS FOR BLIND/VISION-IMPAIRED DOGS:" http://www.olddoghaven.org/

Books:

My Dog is Blind: But Lives Life to the Full! by Nicole Horsky, Pub. Hubble & Hattie, 2010 Veloce Publishing Limited, Veloce House, Parkway Farm Business Park, Poundbury, Dorchester DTI 3AR England. www.hubbleandhattie.com

Living With Blind Dogs by Caroline D. Levin RN, Pub. Lantern Publications, www.petcarebooks.com

---

4   *http://en.wikipedia.org/wiki/Barbara_Woodhouse*

The Winds of Change

This article was written in the 1980s at the request of
The Animals Voice magazine. While progress has been
made since then (at the time this was written, Michael Vick
would not have been arrested, let alone prosecuted), there
is still much to do. Animals still languish in laboratories,
factory farms, and too-small roadside zoo cages. Too many
healthy dogs and cats are still being put to death because
we cannot control their populations or find good homes for
them. Habitats for wild animals are shrinking daily. The
progress should give us hope and energy; the work left to
do should keep us from complacency.

THE SUFFERING OF ANIMALS IS a deep and quiet thing. In
the past, only a few individuals and a handful of cultures
could see it and hear it. The problem was not an absence
of morality or laws, but the size of the circle in which they
were applied. Justice and equality were long accepted as
desirable, indeed necessary, for "civilized society." But they
did not, of course, apply to women, whose rightful place was
in the home (or convent or brothel) under the protection
(subjugation) of men. They certainly did not apply to black
people who were ordained by God to be slaves due to their

inherent need for control and correction. Obviously they could not apply to Jews who were, not only inferior, but deserving of persecution because of their own misdeeds.

Understandably, no one thought to apply them to aboriginal or native peoples who needed taming (stood in the way of material progress) and civilizing. Animals are exempt from just treatment because they need breaking, managing, protecting, and, frequently, killing, and can be used according to human whim because...well, they *need* it—just as women, slaves, Jews, and native peoples *needed* it.

In truth, it was, and is, the needs of the oppressor that were, and are, being fulfilled in excluding all of these groups from the circle of moral consideration, not the needs of the oppressed and excluded. We are witness to the fact that human rights, though far from a reality for all, is now an issue that is taken very seriously.

Years ago, the world watched as the Moskva, a Soviet icebreaker, toiled its way through ice-blocked winter seas to save trapped beluga whales. Ice had closed around the belugas, cutting them off from the open sea, from food, and if the Moskva didn't reach them in time, the ice would cut them off from air. Local human inhabitants fed them by hand and worked around the clock to keep breathing holes open for them. Some of the whales were lost, but the Moskva cut a channel through the ice in time to lead most of them out to sea to the cadences of classical music broadcast over her bow. It was a marvelous outbreak of sanity, sanctioned by the government and carried out with dedication by the people, in a hitherto repressive, whale-killing country.

The wind blowing across Siberia that day carrying the commingled strains of human and whale music was, I like to think, the beginning of Glasnost.

Racism, sexism, anti-Semitism, and homophobia are blinding and deafening. We are more and more able to see and hear the suffering of those who are different from ourselves and to care.

Still, even in the realm of human rights, the steely-eyed realists among us will point out that yes, we have seen the end of human slavery in America, but not, alas, of racism. Women have the vote but remain not quite equal. Native Americans are no longer systematically hunted down or denied the practices of their religions, but despair among many surviving tribes is endemic. The ovens of the Third Reich are cold, but anti-Semitism is rife. In Eastern Europe repressive regimes have crumbled into dust, yet dark patches of tyranny still fester over the globe. And never mind the saving of an occasional whale or the liberation of a handful of laboratory animals, nonhumans are, even as I write these words, even as you read them, being imprisoned, tortured, and killed by the tens of thousands.

Yet...there is a new wind blowing. We may be standing hip-deep in snow, but the light caress of the Chinook is upon our cheeks. Where we stand we are freezing, surrounded by the unbroken landscape of winter, but in the wind is the promise of spring.

And if we listen, we can hear voices on that wind, voices that span the ages, from Moses to Harriet Tubman, Spartacus to Margaret Sanger, from Crazy Horse to Raoul Wallenberg.

These are not just the echoes of saints, though there were saints among them, but of ordinary people who made extraordinary choices—unselfish choices—to further the causes of justice.

And if we look up we will see a galaxy of stars, for even those who are not remembered by name, and those who were swallowed up in the turbulence of their struggles, left their lights. The nameless farmers, merchants, housewives who made up the underground railroad for escaping slaves; the men and women beaten and killed as they defied the British in India to make salt; the Righteous Gentiles who saved Jewish men, women, and children from the Nazis— the galaxy is infinite and filled with lights.

And if we gaze long enough we will see a new constellation in the corner of the sky, not yet as bright as the others, but sharing some of their brightest stars: Gandhi, George Bernard Shaw, Leo Tolstoy, Leonardo Da Vinci, Henry Bergh, and a host of others who made incalculable contributions to enrich humankind and were outspoken in their concern for nonhumans. This galaxy of lights, these voices on the wind, belong to our mothers and fathers. The animal rights movement is the logical outcome of the evolution of human consciousness and expanding compassion.

And when we get discouraged because our movement is still young and we have, as yet, no hindsight to guide us, we can look up and listen and take heart that we can overcome the outside pressures and prejudices and maybe even the internal strife that tends to dim our purpose—that of improving the lives of animals here and now and for the future.

We must keep working with hope and courage for we have proof from the human rights movements that, though we may not immediately change hearts and minds, we can change what people are allowed to do and get away with. The wind is rising, and we are, as yet, but a dim constellation in a galaxy of stars. But without us there would be a dark empty space in the spring sky.

A Circle of Stones

(Dian Fossey b. 1932 d. 1985)

A CIRCLE OF STONES ON a misty mountain marks the grave of a difficult woman; and before its next great adventure, a spirit lingers for a while, mingling with the mist, close as breath to the great gentle ones she loved and refrained from embracing in life.

Death Angel

IF THERE IS AN ANGEL of death, I believe it has the brightest face, the kindest eye, and the softest wing.

About Paulette Callen

PAULETTE CALLEN'S FIRST NOVEL *CHARITY* WAS published by Simon and Schuster in 1997. Since then, she has written three other novels: *Command of Silence*, *Death Can Be Murder*, and *Fervent Charity* (the sequel to *Charity*, published late summer 2013, along with a re-issue of *Charity*, by Ylva Publishing).

Her poems, articles, and short stories have appeared in small journals, magazines, and anthologies. The poem "See, Nadia!" was included in *Beyond Lament, Poets of the World Bearing Witness to the Holocaust* (Northwestern University Press) and was subsequently selected by artist Carol Rosen for inclusion in her *Holocaust Series*, an eight-book collection of photo/text collages housed in the Whitney Museum, the Simon Wiesenthal Center, and the University of Tel Aviv.

Paulette's employment history includes the Communications Department of a large corporation, a movie theatre, a bank, the gift industry, the ASPCA, the insurance sector, as well as summer stock theatres and a year-long stint with a comedy improvisation company. For nearly four years, she served as a volunteer staff member for POWARS (Pet Owners with Aids Resource Services) in New York City.

After many years as a resident of Manhattan's Upper West Side, she has returned, with her rescued blind Shih Tzu Lily, to her hometown in South Dakota.

CONNECT WITH THIS AUTHOR:
Website: www.paulettecallen.com

Other Books by Ylva Publishing

www.ylva-publishing.com

Charity

(revised edition)

Paulette Callen

ISBN: 978-3-95533-075-0

Length: 334 pages

The friendship between Lena Kaiser, a sodbuster's daughter, and Gustie Roemer, an educated Easterner, is unlikely in any other circumstance but post-frontier Charity, South Dakota. Gustie is considered an outsider, and Lena is too proud to share her problems (which include a hard-drinking husband) with anyone else.

On the nearby Sioux reservation, Gustie also finds love and family with two Dakotah women: Dorcas Many Roads, an old medicine woman, and her adopted granddaughter, Jordis, who bears the scars of the white man's education.

When Lena's husband is arrested for murdering his father and the secrets of Gustie's past follow her to Charity, Lena, Gustie, and Jordis stand together. As buried horrors are unearthed and present tragedies unfold, they discover the strength and beauty of love and friendship that blossom like wild flowers in the tough prairie soil.

Fervent Charity

Paulette Callen

ISBN: 978-3-95533-079-8
Length: 337 pages

Fervent Charity continues the story of the friendship of five women who have nothing in common but the ground they walk on and the vicissitudes of post-frontier prairie life.

Lena, a young mother living on the edge of heartbreak. Her sister-in-law, Mary, more beautiful than loved. Alvinia, midwife to the county and mother of ten. Gustie and Jordis, trying to make a home together but finding their place on either the reservation or in Charity precarious.

The women come together in the face of natural hardships—childbirth, disastrous weather, and disease—and the unnatural malevolence of people who mean them harm. In the end, they find themselves bound by a secret none of them could have predicted.

Epiphany
© by Paulette Callen

ISBN: 978-3-95533-364-5

Also available as e-book.

Published by Ylva Publishing, legal entity of Ylva Verlag, e.Kfr.

Ylva Verlag, e.Kfr.
Owner: Astrid Ohletz
Am Kirschgarten 2
65830 Kriftel
Germany

www.ylva-publishing.com

First Edition April 2015

Credits:
Edited by Astrid Ohletz and Nikki Busch
Cover Design by Streetlight Graphics